我的梦想美文
有梦想谁都了不起

英汉对照　词汇解析　语法讲解　励志语录

马琼琼　编著

中国纺织出版社

图书在版编目（CIP）数据

我的梦想美文：有梦想谁都了不起：英文 / 马琼琼编著. -- 北京：中国纺织出版社，2019.5（2020.6重印）

ISBN 978-7-5180-5095-6

Ⅰ.①我… Ⅱ.①马… Ⅲ.①英语—语言读物②散文集—世界 Ⅳ.①H319.4：Ⅰ

中国版本图书馆CIP数据核字（2018）第119977号

责任编辑：武洋洋　　责任印制：储志伟

中国纺织出版社出版发行
地址：北京市朝阳区百子湾东里A407号楼　邮政编码：100124
销售电话：010—67004422　　传真：010—87155801
http://www.c-textilep.com
E-mail:faxing@c-textilep.com
中国纺织出版社天猫旗舰店
官方微博http://www.weibo.com/2119887771
三河市延风印装有限公司印刷　各地新华书店经销
2019年5月第1版　2020年6月第3次印刷
开本：880×1230　1/32　印张：6.25
字数：200千字　定价：39.80元

凡购本书，如有缺页、倒页、脱页，由本社图书营销中心调换

前言

　　思想结晶改变人生命运，经典美文提高生活品位。曾几何时，一个字，触动你的心弦；一句话，让你泪流满面；一篇短文，让你重拾信心，勇敢面对生活给你的考验。这就是语言的魅力。通过阅读优美的英文短文，不仅能够扩大词汇量，掌握单词的用法，了解语法，学习地道的表达，更让你的心灵如沐春风，得到爱的呵护和情感的滋养。

　　岁月流转，经典永存。针对英语学习爱好者的需要，编者精心选取了难易适中的英语经典美文，为你提供一场丰富多彩的文学盛宴。本书采用中英文对照的形式，便于读者理解。每篇美文后都附有单词解析、语法知识点、经典名句三大版块，让你在欣赏完一篇美文后，还能扩充词汇量、巩固语法知识、斟酌文中好句，并感悟人生。在一篇篇不同题材风格的英语美文中，你总能找到引起你心灵共鸣的一篇。

　　读一本新书恰似坠入爱河，是场冒险。你得全身心地投入进去。翻开书页之时，从前言直至封底你或许都知之甚少。但谁又不是呢？字里行间的只言片语不总是正确的。

　　有时候你会发现，人们自我推销时是一种形象，等你在深入了解后，他们就完全变样了。有时故事的叙述流于表面，朴实的语言，平淡的情节，但阅读过半后，你却发觉这本书真是出乎意料的妙不可言，而这种感受只能靠自己去感悟！

阅读之乐，腹有诗书气自华；阅读之美，活水云影共天光。阅读可以放逐百年孤独，阅读可以触摸千年月光。阅读中有眼前的收获，阅读中也有诗和远方。

让我们静下心来感受英语美文的温度，在英语美文中仔细品味似曾相识的细腻情感，感悟生命和人性的力量。

编者
2018年6月

目录

01 No Pain, No Gain
　　没有付出就没有收获 ·· 001

02 Be an Optimist
　　做一个乐观者 ··· 006

03 If the Dream Is Big Enough
　　如果梦想足够远大 ··· 013

04 Happiness Lies in Contentment
　　知足者常乐 ··· 018

05 Follow Your Dream
　　追随梦想 ··· 025

06 Big Rocks in Life
　　人生的大石头 ··· 031

07 Growing Roots
　　成长的树根 ··· 035

08 Run Out of the Rainy Season of Your Life
　　跑出人生的雨季 ··· 042

09 The Shadowland of Dreams
　　美梦难圆 ··· 049

10 Face Adversity with Smile
　　笑对逆境 ··· 054

11 Companionship of Books
　　以书为伴 ··· 059

12 Think Positive Thoughts Every Day
　　积极看待每一天 ··· 065

13 Learn to Live in Reality
学会生活在现实中 ··· 070

14 Extend the Miracle
发挥潜力，创造无限 ··· 076

15 On Achieving Success
论成功 ··· 081

16 Don't Wait for Life to Start
人生莫待绽放 ··· 086

17 Never Too Late to Become What You Want to Be
梦想终有成真时 ·· 092

18 Tiny Steps, Big Changes
寻求大改变，从小处做起 ··· 098

19 Change Your Bad Habit to Good—Modify Your Environment
改掉坏毛病，养成好习惯——改善周边环境 ················· 104

20 Change Your Bad Habit to Good—Monitor Your Behavior
改掉坏毛病，养成好习惯——监督自身行为 ················· 110

21 Change Your Bad Habit to Good—Make Commitments
改掉坏毛病，养成好习惯——许下诺言 ······················· 116

22 We Need Dreams
我们需要梦想 ··· 122

23 What I Have Lived For
我为何而生 ·· 128

24 We're Just Beginning
一切刚开始 ·· 134

25 Sure You Can
相信自己 ··· 140

26 Catch the Star that Holds Your Destiny
抓住生命中的那颗星 ·· 146

27 The Farmer's Donkey
井中之驴 ··· 152

28 Feed Your Mind
   充实你的思想 ··· 157

29 Facing the Enemies Within
   直面内在的敌人 ··· 163

30 On Idleness
   论懒惰 ··· 169

31 Where There Is a Will, There Is a Way
   心中有目标，风雨不折腰 ································ 175

32 Nights
   夜晚 ··· 181

33 The Hard Work Paid Off
   天道酬勤 ··· 187

01 No Pain, No Gain
没有付出就没有收获

Have you ever thought why there are very few great people? I think there is probably only one great person out of 10,000 at best, and most probably much less than that. But why? Most people want to be great, right? Why are there only very few of them? Here is the reason:

Most people do not pay the price of **greatness**.

I think this one is quite **obvious**. Now, the next question is: why not? If there are so many people who want to be great, why only very few of them **actually** pay the price? The answer to these questions explains the difference between the almost 100% people who want to be great and the much less than 0.01% who actually be so.

The reason why very few people actually pay the price is this: The road to greatness is **continuously** painful for long time.

Greatness requires **sacrifices** and there is no sacrifice without pain. The kind of sacrifices required for greatness is the ones that make the process continuously painful for long time. If you want to be good it will be painful

你有没有想过为什么成功的人那么少？我想，大概在一万个人里有一个人能获得成功就很好了。但是为什么会这样呢？我们大多数人都渴望成功，不是吗？那为什么成功的人还是屈指可数呢？原因如下：

大多数人没有为成功付出代价。

这个答案显而易见。那么，就引出了下一个问题：为什么没有呢？为什么有那么多人想要成功，而只有很少数的人愿意为成功付出代价呢？这个问题的答案就能把0.01%真正获得成功的人和几乎是100%想要获得成功的人给区分开来。

极少数人愿意为成功付出代价的真正原因在于：成功之路需要长期痛苦的坚持。

成功要牺牲，而所有的牺牲都伴随着痛苦。获得成功所需要的牺牲是长期的、痛苦的。如果你的目标是优秀，那可能只是"短痛"而已，很多人还是可以承受得住的。但是想要成功，那么所需要承受的就是"长痛"了。大多数人

only every now and then, and many people can still handle it. But being great is a totally different level. The pain is much deeper and it is continuous. Very few people can **endure** this kind of pain and that's why there are very few great people. Most people naturally choose things that bring pleasures to them. It's **unnatural** to choose pain over pleasure, let alone doing it continuously for long time.

But that's what I believe is the secret to greatness: The secret to greatness is choosing pain over pleasures continuously for long time.

会选择能给自己带来快乐的事物，这是自然的选择。很少有人会抛开快乐去选择痛苦，更不用说是长期的痛苦了。

但是正是上述原因让我相信，成功的秘密就在于：选择痛苦而不是快乐，并能够长期坚持承受痛苦。

单词解析 Word Analysis

greatness [ɡreɪtnəs] *n.* 伟大；大；崇高

例 He may not always achieve greatness but at least he's a trier.
他也许并非总能成就大事，但至少他竭尽所能。

obvious [ˈɒbviəs] *adj.* 明显的；显著的

例 It was an obvious mistake for him to have gone alone.
他独自前去是个很明显的错误。

actually [ˈæktʃuəli] *adv.* 实际上；确实；事实上

例 One afternoon, I grew bored and actually fell asleep for a few minutes.
一天下午，我觉得有些无聊，还真的睡着了一小会儿。

No Pain, No Gain
没有付出就没有收获

continuously [kən'tɪnjʊəslɪ] *adv.* 连续不断地，接连地

例 This system continuously monitors levels of radiation and relays the information to a central computer.
这个系统不间断地监控辐射水平，并将信息传送到中央计算机。

sacrifice ['sækrɪfaɪs] *n.* & *v.* 牺牲；献祭，供奉

例 Her husband's pride was a small thing to sacrifice for their children's security.
为了孩子们的安全，舍弃她丈夫的尊严不算什么。

endure [ɪn'djʊə(r)] *vt.* 忍耐；容忍

例 The company endured heavy financial losses.
那家公司遭受了严重亏损。

unnatural [ʌn'nætʃrəl] *adj.* 不自然的，做作的

例 The aircraft rose with unnatural speed on take-off.
那架飞机以反常的速度起飞升空。

语法知识点 Grammar Points

① **The answer to these questions explains the difference between the almost 100% people who want to be great and the much less than 0.01% who actually be so.**

本句中 who 引导定语从句，先行词是 the almost 100% people，先行词在从句中做主语成分；much less than 表示"远小于"。

例 I use watercolors much less than I do oils or acrylics.
我用水彩比用油画颜料或丙烯酸颜料要少得多。
She got much less than she would have done if she had settled out of court.
如果她同意庭外和解的话，得到的肯定会更多。

② **If you want to be good it will be painful only every now and then, and many people can still handle it.**

本句中 if 引导的是个条件状语从句，表示某事很可能发生，条件是可能存在的，主句中某种情况发生的概率也是很高的。

例 If you fail in the exam, you will let him down.
如果你考试不及格，你会让他失望的。

If you have finished the homework, you can go home.
如果你作业做完了就可以回家了。

另外，if 从句还表示不可实现的条件或根本不可能存在的条件，也就是一种虚拟的条件或假设。从句多用一般过去时或过去完成时，表示对现在或过去的一种假设。

例 If I were you, I would invite him to the party.
如果我是你，我会邀请他参加聚会。

I would have arrived much earlier if I had not been caught in the traffic.
要不是交通堵塞，我会来得早一些。

every now and then 表示"有时，时而，不时"。

例 A few cases of influenza cropped out every now and then.
一些流行性感冒的病例不时出现。

Every now and then you hear some bombs bursting.
你会时不时地听到一些爆炸声。

③ **Most people naturally choose things that bring pleasures to them. It's unnatural to choose pain over pleasure, let alone doing it continuously for long time.**

本句中 bring pleasure to sb. 表示"给某人带来快乐"；let alone 表示"更不用说"。

例 When we worship, our goal is to bring pleasure to God, not ourselves.
我们敬拜时，目标是为讨神欢心，而不是让自己开心。

He did not have enough money to have the tire patched up, let alone buy a new one.
他的钱还不够补这个轮胎，更别提买个新的了。

No Pain, No Gain
没有付出就没有收获

经典名句 *Famous Classics*

1. Those who were seen dancing were thought to be insane by those who could not hear the music.
   那些听不见音乐的人认为那些跳舞的人疯了。

2. You have your way. I have my way. As for the right way, the correct way, and the only way, it does not exist.
   你有你的路，我有我的路。至于适当的路、正确的路和唯一的路，这样的路并不存在。

3. A casual stroll through the lunatic asylum shows that faith does not prove anything.
   在疯人院随便逛一下你就能了解，信仰什么也证明不了。

4. Whoever fights monsters should see to it that in the process he does not become a monster. And when you look into the abyss, the abyss also looks into you.
   想要战胜怪物就要了解成为怪物的过程；当你回望无底深渊的时候，无底深渊也会望着你。

5. The true man wants two things: danger and play. For that reason he wants woman, as the most dangerous toy.
   真正的男子汉渴望两件事：危险和游戏。正因为这个原因，他追逐女人——世上最危险的游戏。

6. Those who keep themselves strong will eventually succeed.
   凡是自强不息者，最终都会成功。

7. Miracles sometimes occur, but one has to work terribly for them.
   奇迹有时候是会发生的，但是你得为之拼命地努力。

02 Be an Optimist
做一个乐观者

If you change your mind—from **pessimism** to **optimism**—you can change your life. Do you see the glass as half-full rather than half empty? Do you keep your eye upon the **doughnut**, or upon the hole? Suddenly these clichés are scientific questions, as researchers **scrutinize** the power of positive thinking. Research is proving that optimism can help you to be happier, healthier and more successful. Pessimism leads, by contrast, to hopelessness, sickness and failure, and is linked to **depression**, loneliness and painful shyness. If we could teach people to think more positively, it would be like inoculating them against these mental ills.

Your habits count but the belief that you can succeed affects whether or not you will. In part, that's because optimists and pessimists deal with the same challenges and disappointments in very different ways. When things go wrong the pessimist tends to blame himself. "I'm not good at this." "I always fail." He would say. But the optimist looks for **loopholes**. Negative

如果你能将悲观情绪转化为乐观情绪,那么你将改变自己的命运。你看到的是杯子中的半杯水,还是空着的另一半?你的眼睛盯着的是炸面包圈,还是它当中的圆洞?当研究者们详细检测积极思维的作用时,突然之间这些陈词滥调都成为了科学问题。研究证实,乐观能够让你更加快乐、更加健康、更加成功。相反,悲观则会导致无望、疾病以及挫败;其与消沉、孤独和使人痛苦的腼腆不无关系。假如我们能够教导人们更加积极地去思考,那就会像给他们注射预防这些心理疾病的疫苗。

你的诸多习惯固然重要,但是你能够成功的信念影响着你是否真的会成功。在某种程度上讲,这是由于乐观主义者和悲观主义者以迥异的方式对待相同的挑战与失望。当出了问题之后,悲观主义者往往自我责备。他会说"我不擅长做这种事","我总是失败"。但是乐观主义者则寻找疏漏之处。不管是消极还是积极的想

or positive, it was a self-fulfilling **prophecy**. If people feel hopeless they don't bother to acquire the skills they need to succeed.

A sense of control is the **litmus** test for success. The optimist feels in control of his own life. If things are going badly, he acts quickly, looking for solutions, forming a new plan of action, and reaching out for advice. The pessimist feels like fate's **plaything** and moves slowly. He doesn't seek advice, since he assumes nothing can be done. Many studies suggest that the pessimist's feeling of helplessness **undermines** the body's natural defenses, the **immune** system. Research has found that the pessimist doesn't take good care of himself. Feeling **passive** and unable to **dodge** life's blows, he expects ill health and other misfortunes, no matter what he does. He **munches** on junk food, avoids exercise, ignores the doctor, has another drink.

Most people are a mix of optimism and pessimism, but are inclined in one direction or the other. It is a pattern of thinking learned at our mothers' knees. It grows out of thousands of cautions or encouragements, negative statements or positive ones. Too many "don't" and warnings of danger can make a

法，都是一种本身会得以实现的预言。如果人们感觉毫无希望，那么他们就不会花费力气去获得成功所需要的技能。

有无控制感是成功的试金石。乐观主义者感觉到能够掌握自己的命运。如果事出不利，他立即做出反应，寻求解决办法，制定新的行动计划，而且主动去请教他人。悲观主义者则感觉到自己只能任凭命运摆布，行动起来拖拖拉拉。既然认为无计可施，他便不去寻求他人的意见。许多研究显示，悲观主义者的无助感会损害人体的自然防御体系，即免疫系统。研究发现悲观主义者不会很好地照顾自己。这种人消极被动，不会避开生活中的打击，不管做什么都会担心身体不好或者其他灾祸降临。他吃着垃圾食品，逃避体育锻炼，忽视医生的劝告，总是要再贪一杯。

在大多数人身上，乐观主义和悲观主义兼而有之，但总是更加倾向于其中之一。这是在母亲膝下之时就已经形成的思维模式。它源自千万次警告或者鼓励，积极的或者消极的话语。过多的"不许"和危险警告会让一个孩子感到无能、

child feel incompetent, fearful and pessimistic. Pessimism is a hard habit to break—but it can be done.

胆怯，以至于悲观。悲观是一种很难克服的习惯——但并非不能克服。

单词解析 Word Analysis

pessimism ['pesɪmɪzəm] *n.* 悲观；悲观主义

例 Optimism was gradually taking the place of pessimism.
乐观情绪逐渐取代了悲观主义。

optimism ['ɒptɪmɪzəm] *n.* 乐观；乐观主义

例 Now is the time to forge ahead with all the enthusiasm and optimism that you can manage.
现在到了拿出你最大的热情和积极努力进取的时候了。

doughnut ['dəʊnʌt] *n.* 炸面包圈，圈饼

例 No, I'm going to the snack bar to get a doughnut and some milk.
不，我要到小吃店买一个炸面包圈和一些牛奶。

scrutinize ['skru:tənaɪz] *vt.* 仔细检查

例 Her purpose was to scrutinize his features to see if he was an honest man.
她的目的是通过仔细观察他的相貌以判断他是否诚实。

depression [dɪ'preʃn] *n.* 萎靡不振，沮丧

例 He never forgot the hardships he witnessed during the Great Depression of the 1930s.
他永远不会忘记20世纪30年代经济大萧条时期他所目睹的困苦情形。

loophole ['lu:phəʊl] *n.* 空子；漏洞；观察孔

例 He had found a loophole which allowed him to evade responsibility.
他发现了一个可以让他回避责任的漏洞。

prophecy ['prɒfəsi] *n.* 预言；预言书；预言能力
例 The youth, too, fulfilled the prophecy.
那个年轻人，同样地，让预言说中了。

litmus ['lɪtməs] *n.* 石蕊
例 Ending the fighting must be the absolute priority, the litmus test of the agreements' validity.
停火绝对是第一要务，也是检验协议是否有效的试金石。

plaything ['pleɪθɪŋ] *n.* 玩物，供消遣的东西
例 He would not allow anyone to make him into a political plaything for their own ends.
他不会允许任何人为了达到其自身目的把他变成政治玩物。

undermine [ˌʌndə'maɪn] *v.* 逐渐削弱；使逐步减少效力
例 Offering advice on each and every problem will undermine her feeling of being adult.
对每个问题都给出建议会令她觉得自己不像个成年人。

immune [ɪ'mju:n] *adj.* 免疫的；有免疫力的
例 This blood test will show whether or not you're immune to the disease.
这个血检显示你是否对这种疾病具有免疫力。

passive ['pæsɪv] *adj.* 被动的；消极的
例 His passive attitude made things easier for me.
他顺从的态度让我做起事来要轻松些。

dodge [dɒdʒ] *v.* 闪躲；回避
例 He desperately dodged a speeding car trying to run him down.
他拼命地闪身躲开一辆试图撞倒他的疾驰的汽车。

munch [mʌntʃ] *v.* 用力咀嚼（某物）；大声咀嚼
例 Across the table, his son Benjie munched appreciatively.
桌子对面，他儿子本杰有滋有味地吃着。

我的梦想美文：有梦想谁都了不起

语法知识点 *Grammar Points*

① If you change your mind — from pessimism to optimism — you can change your life.

本句中 if 引导的是一个条件状语从句，句中 change ... from ... to ... 表示"从……变成"，此用法与 change ... from ...into ... 相近，但是后者存在本质上的变化，而前者在强调变化的程度上稍弱。

例 The worm has changed into a butterfly.
这条虫变成了蝴蝶。（完全变化）

The traffic lights change from red to green.
红绿灯从红灯变成了绿灯。（灯没变，光有变化）

② Research is proving that optimism can help you to be happier, healthier and more successful. Pessimism leads, by contrast, to hopelessness, sickness and failure, and is linked to depression, loneliness and painful shyness.

本句中 that 引导宾语从句；句中固定搭配 help sb. (to) do sth. 表示"帮助某人做某事"，to 通常可以省略。

例 We helped her (to) find her things.
我们帮她找东西。

I helped him (to) repair his bike.
我帮他修自行车。

Mother helped me (to) do my homework.
妈妈帮助我做家庭作业。

by contrast 表示"相比之下"。

例 By contrast, social and political tensions might be a bigger worry.
相比之下，社会和政治的紧张局势可能更令人担忧。

③ If we could teach people to think more positively, it would be like inoculating them against these mental ills.

本句中，if 引导条件状语从句；inoculate ... against... 表示"接种预防"。

例 But if the goal is to inoculate us against recession and more financial turmoil, the answer is no.

010

Be an Optimist
做一个乐观者

但是，如果目标是为了防止衰退及避免更多的金融混乱而打防疫针的话，那么答案是否定的。

④ **In part, that's because optimists and pessimists deal with the same challenges and disappointments in very different ways. When things go wrong the pessimist tends to blame himself.**

本句中有较多固定短语，in part 表示"在某种程度上"。

> In part that's because industry is smack in the middle of the city.
> 部分原因在于：工业恰好在城市的中心。

deal with 表示"应付；对待；惠顾；与……交易"，本文中表示"应对，应付"之意。

> In dealing with suicidal youngsters, our aims should be clear.
> 在对待有自杀倾向的青少年时，我们的目标应当很明确。

tend to 表示"趋向；朝某方向；偏重"，本文中表示"倾向于"之意。

> In our culture we tend to be bashful about our talents and skills.
> 在我们的文化中，我们往往羞于谈论自己的才干和技能。

经典名句 Famous Classics

1. Perseverance is failing nineteen times and succeeding the twentieth.
   十九次失败，到第二十次获得成功，这就叫坚持。

2. Soft beaches are the easiest to leave footprints, but also most likely to be wiped out by the tide.
   松软的沙滩上最容易留下脚印，但也最容易被潮水抹去。

3. No matter when you start, it is important that you do not stop after the start.
   不论你在什么时候开始，重要的是开始之后就不要停止。

4. Time goes by so fast, people go in and out of your life. You must never miss the opportunity to tell these people how much they mean to you.
   时间在流逝，生命中人来人往。不要错失机会告诉他们，他们在你生命中的意义。

5. No matter how bad your heart has been broken, the world doesn't stop for your grief. The sun comes right back up the next day.
不管你有多痛苦,这个世界都不会为你停止转动,太阳照样升起。

6. If you would hit the mark, you must aim a little above it. Every arrow that flies feels the attraction of earth. —Henry Wadsworth Longfellow.
要想射中靶心,必须瞄准比靶心略高的位置,因为脱弦之箭都受到地心引力的影响。——亨利·沃兹沃斯·胡费罗

读书笔记

03 If the Dream Is Big Enough
如果梦想足够远大

I used to watch her from my kitchen window, she seemed so small as she **muscled** her way through the crowd of boys on the playground. The school was across the street from our home and I would often watch the kids as they played during **recess**. A sea of children, and yet to me, she stood out from them all. I remember the first day I saw her playing basketball. I watched in wonder as she ran circles around the other kids. She managed to shoot jump shots just over their heads and into the net. The boys always tried to stop her but no one could. I began to notice her at other times, basketball in hand, playing alone. She would practice **dribbling** and shooting over and over again, sometimes until dark.

One day I asked her why she practiced so much. She looked directly in my eyes and without a moment of **hesitation** she said, "I want to go to college. The only way I can go is if I get a scholarship. I like basketball. I decided that if I were good enough, I would get a scholarship. I am going to play college basketball. I want to be the

我以前常常从厨房的窗户看到她，她显得那么小，她强行挤过操场上的一群男生。学校在我家对面的街上，我经常在休息的时候看着孩子们玩耍。一大群孩子，但对我来说，她从他们当中脱颖而出。我记得我第一次看到她在操场上打篮球的时候，她在其他孩子旁边兜来转去，技术娴熟，我感到十分惊奇。她成功地从他们的头上跳投射入。男孩们总是试图阻止她，但没人能阻止得了她。我开始注意到她在其他时候也篮球在手，独自玩耍。她会一遍又一遍地练习运球和投篮，有时直到天黑。

有一天，我问她为什么练习这么多。她直视我的眼睛，毫不犹豫地说："我想上大学。我能去的唯一办法就是拿到奖学金。我喜欢篮球。我认为如果我足够好，我就会获得奖学金。我要去打大学篮球。我想成为最好的。我爸爸告诉我，如果梦想足够大，事实并不重要。"然后她笑着跑向球场开始我看了一遍又一遍常规

best. My Daddy told me if the dream is big enough, the facts don't count." Then she smiled and ran towards the court to **recap** the routine I had seen over and over again. Well, I had to give it to her—she was determined. I watched her through those junior high years and into high school. Every week, she led her **varsity** team to victory. The next year, as she and her team went to the Northern California **Championship** game, she was seen by a college **recruiter**. She was indeed offered a scholarship, a full ride, to a Division I, **NCAA** women's basketball team. She was going to get the college education that she had dreamed of and worked toward for all those years. It's true: If the dream is big enough, the facts don't count.

动作。好吧，我必须承认她真的下定决心了。我看着她通过初中，进入高中。每周我都看着她带领她的代表队获取胜利。第二年，当她和她的球队去参加加利福尼亚北部锦标赛时，她被一个大学招聘人员看到了。她真的得到了奖学金，全额奖学金，在NCAA女子篮球队。她将接受她曾梦想并为之奋斗多年的大学教育。这是真的：如果梦想足够大，事实并不重要。

单词解析 Word Analysis

muscle ['mʌsl] *n.* 肌肉；力量；权威，权力 *vt.* 硬挤；使劲搬动 *vi.* 用力挤

例 Keeping your muscles strong and in tone helps you to avoid back problems.
保持肌肉强壮发达有利于预防背部疾病。

recess [rɪ'ses] *n.* 休息；隐蔽处；（山脉，海岸等的）凹处；壁凹，壁龛

例 The conference broke for a recess.
会议暂时休会。

dribbling ['drɪblɪŋ] *v.* 运球，带球

例 I have no doubt of his basic skills in passing, dribbling and shooting.

If the Dream Is Big Enough
如果梦想足够大 03

我丝毫不怀疑他传球、运球和射门的基本技术。

hesitation [ˌhezɪˈteɪʃn] *n.* 犹豫；踌躇；含糊；口吃

例 He promised there would be no more hesitations in pursuing reforms.
他答应在推进改革这件事上不再迟疑不决。

recap [ˈriːkæp] *v.* 翻新（轮胎）的胎面；扼要重述，概括

例 To recap briefly, an agreement negotiated to cut the budget deficit was rejected 10 days ago.
简要概括起来，一项关于削减预算赤字的协议在10天前遭到了否决。

varsity [ˈvɑːsəti] *n.* 大学（尤指牛津或剑桥）；（学校的）代表队

例 The school has not given them the same opportunities to participate in varsity sports that men receive.
学校没有给她们与男生同样多的参加大学体育活动的机会。

championship [ˈtʃæmpiənʃɪp] *n.* 锦标赛，冠军赛；冠军头衔，冠军称号

例 This season I expect us to retain the championship and win the European Cup.
这个赛季我期待我们能够保住冠军头衔，赢得欧洲杯。

recruiter [rɪˈkruːtə(r)] *n.* 招聘人员，征兵人员

例 If you don't know the recruiter's name, simply list the company name and address.
如果你不知道招聘员工的名字，简单地写上公司名字和地址吧。

NCAA *abbr.* National Collegiate Athletic Association <美>全国大学生体育协会

例 NCAA games is one of the biggest and the highest level games in the world.
美国大学生篮球联赛是世界上规模最大、水平最高的大学生篮球联赛之一。

我的梦想美文：有梦想谁都了不起

语法知识点 *Grammar Points*

① A sea of children, and yet to me, she stood out from them all.

本句中 stand out of 为固定搭配，表示"突出；坚持；超群；向前跨步"。

例 Only in this way can we avoid the adverse effects, stand out of the hardship and seek development and success.
这样，我们才能避免不利的影响，在困境中脱颖而出，寻求发展和成功。

② I watched in wonder as she ran circles around the other kids.

本句中 run circles around 为固定搭配，表示"兜来转去"，还有引申意为"比（某人）做得更好，远远超过（某人）"。

例 I'm a far better player than my opponent. I can run circles around him.
我的球技比我的对手好得多，我可以把他耍得团团转。

③ Every week, she led her varsity team to victory.

本句中 lead sb. to victory 为固定搭配，表示"带领某人走向胜利"。

例 I will lead us to victory.
我会引领我们走向胜利。

④ The next year, as she and her team went to the Northern California Championship game, she was seen by a college recruiter.

本句中，as 引导的是一个时间状语从句，表示"当……时候"；同时 as 还可以引导定语从句、原因状语从句、方式状语从句和让步状语从句。

例 As the weather is colder and colder, the leaves of the tree is less and less.
随着天气越来越冷，树叶变得越来越少。

⑤ She was going to get the college education that she had dreamed of and worked toward for all those years.

本句中，that 引导的是一个定语从句，先行词是 education。此处可以用 which 替代。

If the Dream Is Big Enough
如果梦想足够大

经典名句 Famous Classics

1. Sometimes you have to let things go, so there's room for better things to come into your life.
   有时你要学会放手,这样才有空间让更好的事物进入你的生活。

2. Never get stuck with the thing that ruins your day. Stay upbeat and be happy; for life is too short to be wasted on crap.
   不要让不好的事情毁了你这一天,乐观一点,开心一点,生命如此短暂,别浪费时间在不值一提的事情上。

3. Lies will always be bitter in the end, no matter how sweet you made it at the beginning.
   到最后,谎言总是苦涩的,不管开始的时候是多么的悦耳。

4. Always remember: when the pain of holding on is greater than the pain of letting go, it's time to let go.
   记住:当坚持之苦大过放弃之痛,是该放手的时候了。

5. Many of life's failures are people who did not realize how close they were to success when they gave up.
   我们生活中的许多失败,是因为人们在放弃的时候没有认识到他们距离成功有多么近。

6. I don't need a photograph to recall you, because you've never left my mind.
   我不需要一张照片把你记起,因为在我脑海中你从未离去。

7. When all else is lost the future still remains.
   即使失去了一切,还有未来。

读书笔记

04 Happiness Lies in Contentment
知足者常乐

Many people believe that they will be happy once they arrive at some **specific** goal they set for themselves. However, more often than not, once you arrive "there" you will still feel **dissatisfied**, and move your "there" vision to yet another point in the future. By always chasing after another "there," you are never really appreciating what you already have right "here." It is important for human beings to keep sober-minded about the age-old drive to look beyond the place where you now stand. On one hand, your life is enhanced by your dreams and aspirations. On the other hand, these drives can pull you farther and farther from your **enjoyment** of your life right now. By learning the lessons of **gratitude** and **abundance**, you can bring yourself closer to fulfilling the **challenge** of living in the present.

Gratitude means you are thankful for and **appreciative** of what you have and where you are on your path right now. Gratitude fills your heart with the joyful feeling and allows you to fully appreciate everything that arises on your path. As

许多人都相信，一旦他们达到了自己所设定的某个特定目标，他们就会开心、快乐。然而事实往往是，当你到达彼岸时，你还是不知足、不满意，而且又有了新的彼岸——新的幻想和憧憬。由于你总是疲于追逐一个又一个的彼岸，你从未真正欣赏、珍惜你已经拥有的一切。不安于现状的欲望人皆有之，由来已久，但重要的是要对它保持清醒的头脑。一方面，你的生活因为梦想和渴望而更加精彩。另一方面，这些欲望又使你越来越不懂得珍惜和享受现在拥有的生活。假如你能懂得感恩，学会知足，你就接近实现生活在现实中提出的要求。

感恩之心是指你感激、珍惜自己当前所拥有的一切以及所处的人生境遇。心存感恩，你的心灵就充满愉悦，你就能真正领会人生路上的种种体验。如果你努力把眼光锁定在此时此刻，你就能感受它的美妙之处。

许多方法可以培育感恩之

Happiness Lies in Contentment
知足者常乐

you strive to keep your focus on the present moment, you can experience the full wonder of "here."

There are many ways to **cultivate** gratitude. Here are just a few suggestions you may wish to try:

1. Imagine what your life would be like if you lost all that you had. This will most surely remind you of how much you do appreciate it.

2. Make a list each day of all that you are grateful for, so that you can stay conscious daily of your **blessings**. Do this especially when you are feeling as though you have nothing to feel grateful for. Or spend a few minutes before you go to sleep, giving thanks for all that you have.

3. Spend time offering **assistance** to those who are less **fortunate** than you, so that you may gain perspective.

However you choose to learn gratitude is irrelevant. What really matters is that you create a space in your consciousness for appreciation for all that you have right now, so that you may live more joyously in your present moment.

One of the most common human fears is scarcity. Many people are afraid of not having enough of what they need or want, and so they are always striving to get to a point when they would finally have enough.

心,你不妨试试以下几种:

1.设想如果你失去了你现在所拥有的一切,你的生活将会怎么样。它肯定会使你回想起原来你是多么喜欢和珍视这一切。

2.每天都列出那些值得你感激的事物,那样你就能时时刻刻意识到自己的幸运。每天都要这么做,尤其是当你觉得好像没有什么可感激的时候。另外你也可以每天临睡前花几分钟感恩自己所拥有的一切。

3.花时间帮助那些没有你那么幸运的人,这样你也许会对生活有正确的认识。

其实,你选择何种方法去学会感恩,这无关紧要,真正重要的是你应该有意识地努力去欣赏和珍视你现在所拥有的一切,这样你就可以更快乐地享受你目前的生活。

贫穷是人类最普遍的恐惧之一。许多人担心自己的所需所求不够,所以他们总是孜孜以求有朝一日能心满意足,别无他求。

贫穷感可以归因于"精神空虚综合征",即我们试图用身外之物来填补内心的空缺。但是,就像拼图游戏一样,你不能把本来不属于那个地方的

Scarcity consciousness arises as a result of the "hole-in-the-soul **syndrome**." This is when we attempt to fill the gaps in our inner lives with things from the outside world. But like puzzle pieces, you can't fit something in where it does not naturally belong. No amount of external objects, **affection**, love, or attention can ever fill an inner void. We already have enough, so we should revel in our own **interior** abundance.

东西硬塞进去。任何身外之物、情感、关爱和关注都无法填补内心的空虚。我们拥有的已经足够，因此我们应该满足于内心世界的丰富与充实。

单词解析 Word Analysis

specific [spəˈsɪfɪk] *adj.* 具体的；明确的

例 Massage may help to increase blood flow to specific areas of the body.
按摩有助于增加身体特定部位的血液流量。

dissatisfied [dɪsˈsætɪsfaɪd] *adj.* 感到不满的，不满意的，不高兴的

例 82% of voters are dissatisfied with the way their country is being governed.
82%的选民对本国的治理方式不满意。

enjoyment [ɪnˈdʒɔɪmənt] *n.* 享受；享有；令人愉快的事物

例 I apologize if your enjoyment of the movie was spoiled.
如果破坏了你看电影的兴致，我道歉。

gratitude [ˈɡrætɪtjuːd] *n.* 谢意；感激，感谢

例 I wish to express my gratitude to Kathy Davis for her immense practical help.
凯茜·戴维斯实实在在地帮了大忙，我想对她表示感谢。

Happiness Lies in Contentment
知足者常乐 04

abundance [ə'bʌndəns] *n.* 丰度；丰富，充裕
- 例 The area has an abundance of wildlife.
  这片地区有丰富的野生动植物。

challenge ['tʃæləndʒ] *n.* 挑战；质疑
- 例 I like a big challenge and they don't come much bigger than this.
  我喜欢大的挑战，而所有挑战中再没有比这更大的了。

appreciative [ə'priːʃətɪv] *adj.* 感激的；有欣赏力的
- 例 Mrs. Hastings's eyes grow warmer and more appreciative with my every word.
  我讲的每句话让黑斯廷斯夫人的眼神变得越来越热情，越来越充满欣赏。

cultivate ['kʌltɪveɪt] *v.* 教养；栽培；改善；交朋友
- 例 He has written eight books and has cultivated the image of an elder statesman.
  他已经写了8本书，树立起了其政界元老的形象。

blessing ['blesɪŋ] *n.* 祝福；好事；福分
- 例 Rivers are a blessing for an agricultural country.
  河流对于一个农业国家来说是一种恩赐。

assistance [ə'sɪstəns] *n.* 帮助，援助
- 例 Since 1976 he has been operating the shop with the assistance of volunteers.
  从1976年开始，他就在志愿者的帮助下经营这个店。

fortunate ['fɔːtʃənət] *adj.* 侥幸的，幸运的
- 例 Central London is fortunate in having so many large parks and open spaces.
  伦敦市中心有幸拥有许多大型公园和大片空地。

syndrome ['sɪndrəum] *n.* 综合征；综合症状
- 例 Irritable bowel syndrome seems to affect more women than men.
  女性比男性更易患肠易激综合征。

affection [əˈfekʃn] *n.* 喜爱，爱慕；情感；意向

例　I cherish for you the liveliest feeling of affection and gratitude.
我对你怀有最强烈的爱和感激之情。

interior [ɪnˈtɪəriə(r)] *adj.* 内部的；内地的

例　The interior of the house was furnished with heavy, old-fashioned pieces.
房子里摆放着笨重的旧式家具。

语法知识点 *Grammar Points*

① **However, more often than not, once you arrive "there" you will still feel dissatisfied, and move your "there" vision to yet another point in the future.**

本句中 once 引导时间状语从句，表示"一旦"。

例　The decision had taken about 10 seconds once he'd read a market research study.
在他看过一份市场调研报告后大概10秒钟就做出了决定。

Once customers come to rely on these systems they almost never take their business elsewhere.
顾客一旦依赖上这些系统，几乎就不会光顾其他商家。

more often than not 表示"往往，多半"。

例　More often than not, he's drunk when I meet him.
每当我见到他时，他通常是喝得醉醺醺的。

Ben is a fairly good runner, he wins more often than not.
本是个相当不错的赛跑选手，他常常跑赢。

② **On the one hand, your life is enhanced by your dreams and aspirations. On the other hand, these drives can pull you farther and farther from your enjoyment of your life right now.**

本句中 on the one hand...on the other hand...表示"一方面……另一方面……"。

例　The carrying out of Putonghua Proficiency Test can check the result of Putonghua teaching on the one hand; on the other

Happiness Lies in Contentment
知足者常乐 04

hand, it can give more inspiration to the further development of Putonghua teaching.

普通话水平测试工作的逐步展开，一方面对普通话教学的成果予以检测，另一方面，也给普通话教学工作的进一步开展以多方面的启示。

③ **As you strive to keep your focus on the present moment, you can experience the full wonder of "here."**

本句中，as 引导的是一个时间状语从句，表示"当……时"；keep focus on 表示"保持关注"。

例 Always keep focus on the social and public affairs, play an important role of monitoring and promoting the healthy development of the society.

时刻保持对社会公共事务的关注，发挥监督和促进社会良性发展的重要作用。

④ **Spend time offering assistance to those who are less fortunate than you, so that you may gain perspective.**

本句中 who 引导定语从句，先行词是 those，who 引导定语从句先行词可以是人、人格化了的动物、神话故事中的人物或有生命的事物；so that 引导结果状语从句。

例 The dog who is barking is our pet.
正在叫的那条狗是我们的宠物。
He spoke at the top of his voice, so that the students at the back heard him.
他说话声音很高，所以后面的同学都听见了。

经典名句 Famous Classics

1. Our destiny offers not the cup of despair, but the chalice of opportunity. So let us seize it, not in fear, but in gladness.
命运给予我们的不是失望之酒，而是机会之杯。因此，让我们毫无畏惧，满心愉悦地把握命运。

2. Success is the ability to go from one failure to another with no

loss of enthusiasm.
成功是，你即使跨过一个又一个失败，但也没有失去热情。

3. Whatever is worth doing is worth doing well.
   任何值得做的，就把它做好。

4. All the unpleasant things, in the end is a good thing.
   所有不如意的事，到最后都是好事。

5. To conquer the world, is not great; a person can conquer himself, is the greatest person in the world.
   征服世界，并不伟大；一个人能征服自己，才是世界上最伟大的人。

读书笔记

05 Follow Your Dream
追随梦想

There was a young man born in a poor family. As a result, his school career was **continually interrupted**. Once he was asked to write a paper about what he wanted to be and do when he grew up. That night he wrote a seven-page paper describing his goal of someday owning a horse **ranch**. He wrote about his dream in great detail and he even drew a **diagram** of a 200-**acre** ranch. Then he drew a detailed floor plan for a 4,000-square-foot house that would sit on a 200-acre dream ranch. He put a great deal of his heart into the project and the next day he handed it in to his teacher.

Two days later, he received his paper back. On the front page was a large red F with a note that read, "See me after class." The boy with the dream went to see the teacher after class and asked, "Why did I receive an F?" The teacher said, "This is an **unrealistic** dream for a young boy like you. You have no money. You have no resources from your family. There's no way you could ever do it." Then the teacher added, "If you will rewrite this paper with a more realistic goal, I will

有一个年轻人出生在一个贫穷的家庭里。因此，他的求学过程并不顺利。一次他被要求写一篇关于当他长大后想做什么的作业。那天晚上，他写了七页纸，描述他的目标是将来拥有一个大马场。他详细地写下了他的梦想，甚至还画了一张200亩农场的设计图。他详尽地计划4000平方英尺的房子，坐落在一个200亩农场的梦想。他一心一意完成这个项目并在第二天交给了老师。

两天后他拿回了报告。封面上是一个又红又大的F和一个便条。"下课后来见我。"怀着梦想的男孩下课后去见老师，他问："为什么给我不及格？"老师说："这是一个不切实际的梦想。一个小孩像你，没有钱，没有来自家庭的资源，你没有办法做到。"接着他又说："如果你重新写一个比较现实的目标，我会重新考虑你的分数。"

男孩回到家里，思考了很久。他问他的父亲他应该怎么做。他的父亲说："听着，儿

reconsider your grade."

The boy went home and thought about it long and hard. He asked his father what he should do. His father said, "Look, son, you have to make up your own mind on this. However, I think it is a very important decision for you." Finally, after sitting with it for a week, the boy turned in the same paper, making no changes at all. He stated, "You can keep the F and I'll keep my dream."

Recollecting the story, my friend Monty and I are now sitting in his 4, 000-square-foot house in the middle of a 200-acre horse ranch. Two summers ago, that same school teacher brought 30 kids to camp out on his ranch. When the teacher was leaving, he said, "Look, Monty, I can tell you this now. When I was your teacher, I was something of a dream **stealer**. During those years I stole a lot of kids' dreams. Fortunately you had enough **gumption** not to give up on yours."

Don't let anyone steal your dreams. Follow your heart, no matter what.

子，在这上面你必须自己做决定。然而，我认为这是一个非常重要的决定。"小男孩对着那个作业静坐了一个星期后，他并没有做任何改动，又重新提交了。他说，"你可以给我F，我会坚持我的梦想。"

回忆着这个故事，我的朋友和我正坐在他的占地4000平方英尺的房子中间，一个200英亩的牧场上。两年前的夏天，那位老师带了30个孩子在他的农场露营。当老师离开的时候，他说："看，蒙蒂，我现在可以告诉你了。当我是你老师的时候，我是一个梦想的小偷。在那些年里，我偷走了很多孩子们的梦想。幸亏你有这个毅力坚持自己的梦想。"

不要让任何人偷走你的梦想。无论如何，追随你的梦想。

单词解析 Word Analysis

continually [kən'tɪnjuəli] *adv.* 不断地；频繁地

例 His wife kept continually dinning in his ear.
他老婆不断地在他耳朵边唠叨。

Follow Your Dream 追随梦想

interrupt [ˌɪntəˈrʌpt] v. 打断；打扰；中断；阻碍

例 The sudden noise from the next room interrupted my train of thinking.
从隔壁房间突然传来的吵闹声打断了我的思路。

ranch [ræntʃ] n. 牧场

例 It's about 50 kilometers from here to my ranch.
从这儿到我的牧场约有五十公里。

diagram [ˈdaɪəɡræm] n. 图解；图表

例 She gave me a diagram of railway network.
她给了我一张铁路图。

acre [ˈeɪkər] n. 英亩

例 We own 100 acres of farmland.
我们拥有一百英亩农田。

unrealistic [ˌʌnriːəˈlɪstɪk] adj. 不切实际的；不实在的

例 The proposal struck me as unrealistic.
我感到这个建议不现实。

recollect [ˌrekəˈlekt] v. 回忆；回想；记起

例 He is able to clearly recollect her looking.
他可以很清楚地回忆起她的容貌。

stealer [stiːlər] n. 偷取者

例 He is a heart stealer.
他是个偷心贼。

gumption [ˈɡʌmpʃn] n. 机智；精明；魄力；进取心

例 He's a nice enough lad, but he doesn't seem to have much gumption.
他是个不错的小伙子，但好像没有什么进取心。

语法知识点 Grammar Points

① He wrote about his dream in great detail and he even drew a diagram of a 200-acre ranch.

027

in great detail 非常详细地

例 They cast their plan in great detail.
他们制订了非常具体的计划。

He could remember every trivial incident in great detail.
他能把每件小事的细节都记得很清楚。

diagram of ……的关系图

例 Draw a diagram of your immediate family.
绘制您的直系亲属图。

The engineer drew a diagram of the bridge.
工程师绘制了一幅这座桥的示意图。

② He put a great deal of his heart into the project and the next day he handed it in to his teacher.

put sth. into 把某物放进……

例 He put all his redundancy money into a shop.
他把所有剩余资金都投入了一家商店。

put into 输入；使进入；把……译成；表达

例 In recent years a number of communications satellites have been put into orbit.
近些年来，很多通信卫星被送上轨道。

The deceiver was put into prison.
那个骗子被关进监狱。

a great deal of 许多的；大量的（后接不可数名词）

例 They eat a great deal of fruit in addition.
他们还吃大量的水果。

hand in 交上；递交

例 Please hand in your paper before June 30th.
请在六月三十日前交论文。

He held up his hand in amazement.
他惊骇地举起了手。

③ His father said, "Look, son, you have to make up your own mind on this".

make up mind 下决心，决定做某事例 She made up mind that, no matter what may come, she would stay there.
她下定决心，不管发生什么情况，她都要在那里待下去。
The city government office makes up mind to widen roads and actively plans to build the subway in the whole city.
市政府下决心在全市范围内拓宽道路并积极筹划修建地铁。

④ When I was your teacher, I was something of a dream stealer.
这个句子中有一个when引导的时间状语从句。
something of 有几分；在某种程度上

例 I'm something of an expert on antiques.
我对古董略有研究。
I've known him for many years, but he remains something of an enigma to me.
我与他相识多年，他仍然难以捉摸。

经典名句 Famous Classics

1. We are all in the gutter, but some of us are looking at the stars.
   我们都生活在阴沟，但仍有些人仰望星空。

2. The tragedy of life doesn't lie in not reaching your goal. The tragedy lies in having no goal to reach.
   人生的悲剧不是没有实现目标，而是没有目标可实现。

3. A kiss can be a comma, a question mark or an exclamation point. That's basic spelling that every woman ought to know.
   一个亲吻也许是一个逗号，一个问号或者一个惊叹号。每个女人都应该明白这些基本拼写。

4. Who would give a law to lovers? Love is unto itself a higher law.
   谁会给爱侣们立法呢？爱情本身就是更高的法则。

5. Don't be afraid to encounter risks. It is by taking chances that we learn how to be brave.
   不要害怕冒险，正是这一机遇才教会我们勇敢。

6. Life can only be understood backwards, but it must be lived forwards.
只有向后看才能理解生活；但要生活得好，则必须向前看。

7. Yesterday is history. Tomorrow is a mystery and Today is a gift: that's why we call it "The Present".
昨天已成为历史，明天神秘而不可知，今天则是一个礼物，所以我们把它叫"现在"（礼物）。

读书笔记

06 Big Rocks in Life
人生的大石头

One day, an expert in time **management** was speaking to a group of students and, to drive home a point, used an **illustration** those students will never forget.

As he stood in front of the group of **overachievers** he said, "OK, time for a quiz." He pulled out a one-gallon, wide-mouth jar and set it on the table in front of him. He also produced about a dozen fist-sized rocks and carefully placed them, one at a time, into the jar. When the jar was filled to the top and no more rocks would fit inside, he asked, "Is this jar full?"

Everyone in the class yelled, "Yes." The time management expert replied, "Really?" He reached under the table and pulled out a bucket of **gravel**. He **dumped** some gravel in and shook the jar, causing pieces of gravel to work themselves down into the spaces between the big rocks. He then asked the group once more, "Is this jar full?"

By this time the class was on to him. "Probably not, " one of them answered. "Good!" he replied. He reached under the table and brought out a bucket of sand. He started dumping

一天，时间管理专家为一群学生讲课。他现场做了演示，给学生们留下了一生都难以磨灭的印象。

站在那些高智商高学历的学生前面，他说："我们来做个小测验。"他拿出一个一加仑的广口瓶放在面前的桌上。随后，他取出一堆拳头大小的石块，仔细地一块一块放进玻璃瓶。直到石块高出瓶口，再也放不下了，他问道："瓶子满了吗？"

所有学生应道："满了！"时间管理专家反问："真的？"他伸手从桌下拿出一桶碎石，倒了一些进去，并敲击玻璃瓶壁使碎石填满下面石块的间隙。"现在瓶子满了吗？"他第二次问道。

这一次学生们有些明白了，"可能还没有。"一位学生应道。"很好！"专家说。他伸手从桌下拿出一桶沙子，开始慢慢倒进玻璃瓶。沙子填满了石块和碎石的所有间隙。他又一次问学生："瓶子满了吗？"

"没满！"学生们大声说。他再一次："很好！"然后他拿

the sand in the jar and it went into all of the spaces left between the rocks and the gravel. Once more he asked the question, "Is this jar full?"

"No!" the class shouted. Once again he said, "Good." Then he grabbed a **pitcher** of water and began to pour it in until the jar was filled to the brim. Then he looked at the class and asked, "What is the point of this illustration?" One **eager** student raised his hand and said, "The point is, no matter how full your **schedule** is, if you try really hard you can always fit some more things in it!"

"No, " the speaker replied, "that's not the point. The truth this illustration teaches us is if you don't put the big rocks in first, you'll never get them in at all. What are the 'big rocks' in your life? Time with your loved ones, your education, your dreams, a worthy cause, teaching or **mentoring** others? Remember to put these big rocks in first or you'll never get them in at all."

过一壶水倒进玻璃瓶直到水面与瓶口平。抬头看着学生，问道："这个例子说明什么？"一个心急的学生举手发言："无论你的时间多少，如果你确实努力，你可以做更多的事情！"

"不！"时间管理专家说，"那不是它真正的重点。这个例子告诉我们，如果你不是先放大石块，那你就再也不能把它放进瓶子里了。那么，什么是你生命中的大石头呢？陪伴你爱的人、学历、梦想、崇高的事业、教育指导其他人？切记，先填满大石头，否则你永远都没法再放入大石头了。"

单词解析 Word Analysis

management [ˈmænɪdʒmənt] *n.* 管理；管理人员

例 The zoo needed better management rather than more money.
这座动物园需要更好的管理，而不是更多的资金。

Big Rocks in Life 人生的大石头 06

illustration [ˌɪləˈstreɪʃn] *n.* 插图；说明；例证；图解
例 To give a definition of a word is more difficult than to give an illustration of its use.
给一个词下定义要比举例说明它的用法困难得多。

overachiever [ˌəʊvərəˈtʃiːvə(r)] *n.* 优等生；高成就者
例 I would love for people to think of me as a talented overachiever.
我想让人承认我的天赋，更希望他们肯定我的努力。

gravel [ˈɡrævl] *n.* 砾石；沙砾，碎石
例 The gravel pits have been landscaped and planted to make them attractive to wildfowl.
砾石采掘坑已进行了景观美化并种上草木，希望能吸引野禽的到来。

dump [dʌmp] *vt.* 倾倒
例 We dumped our bags at the nearby Grand Hotel and hurried towards the market.
我们把包扔在附近的格兰德酒店后就匆匆赶往集市。

pitcher [ˈpɪtʃə(r)] *n.* 大水罐；投掷的人
例 As a pitcher, John is better than James by a long chalk.
作为一名棒球投手，约翰比詹姆斯高明得多。

eager [ˈiːɡə(r)] *adj.* 渴望的；热切的
例 Arty sneered at the crowd of eager faces around him.
阿蒂对他身边那些期盼的面孔嗤之以鼻。

schedule [ˈʃedjuːl] *n.* 预定计划
例 He has been forced to adjust his schedule.
他被迫调整了自己的日程安排。

mentor [ˈmentɔː(r)] *vt.* 指导
例 She says you could also identify useful members of management and ask them to mentor you.
她说，你还可以在管理层内找到一些对你有用的人，请他们指导你。

语法知识点 Grammar Points

① **One day, an expert in time management was speaking to a group of students and, to drive home a point, used an illustration those students will never forget.**

本句中 drive home a point 表示"清晰地阐述一个论点"。

例　To drive his home point, he explained it again.
　　为了讲清楚自己的观点，他又解释了一遍。

② **The truth this illustration teaches us is if you don't put the big rocks in first, you'll never get them in at all.**

本句中，that 引导定语从句：the truth (that) this illustration teaches us...，先行词在从句中做宾语成分，that 可省略；if 引导条件状语从句。

例　This is the TV set (that) my father bought last year.
　　这是我父亲去年买的电视机。

经典名句 Famous Classics

1. Sometimes one pays most for the things one gets for nothing.
有时候一个人为不花钱得到的东西付出的代价最高。

2. To travel hopefully is a better thing than to arrive, and the true success is to labor.
怀着希望去旅行比抵达目的地更愉快；而真正的成功在于工作。

3. I might say that success is won by three things: first, effort; second, more effort; third, still more effort.
可以说成功要靠三件事才能赢得：努力，努力，再努力。

4. Only those who have the patience to do simple things perfectly ever acquire the skill to do difficult things easily.
只有有耐心圆满完成简单工作的人，才能够轻而易举地完成困难的事。

5. The important thing in life is to have a great aim, and the determination to attain it.
人生之要事在于确立伟大的目标与实现这目标的决心。

07 Growing Roots
成长的树根

When I was growing up, I had an old neighbor named Dr. Gibbs. He didn't look like any doctor I'd ever known. He never **yelled** at us for playing in his yard. I remember him as someone who was a lot nicer than **circumstances** warranted.

When Dr. Gibbs wasn't saving lives, he was planting trees. His house sat on ten acres, and his life's goal was to make it a forest.

The good doctor had some interesting theories concerning plant **husbandry**. He came from the "No pain, no gain" school of **horticulture**. He never watered his new trees, which flew in the face of conventional wisdom. Once I asked why. He said that watering plants **spoiled** them, and that if you water them, each **successive** tree generation will grow weaker and weaker. So you have to make things rough for them and weed out the **weenie** trees early on.

He talked about how watering trees made for **shallow** roots, and how trees that weren't watered had to grow deep roots in search of moisture. I took

在我还是小孩子的时候，我有一个老邻居叫吉布斯医生。他不像我所认识的任何一个医生。我们在他的院子里玩耍，他从不对我们大喊大叫。我记得他是一个非常和蔼的人。

吉布斯医生不拯救人性命的时候就去种树。他的住所占地10英亩，他的人生目标就是将它变成一片森林。

这个好医生对于如何持家有一番有趣的理论。他来自一个"不劳无获"的园艺学校。他从不浇灌他新种的树，这显然与常理相悖。有一次我问为什么，他说浇水会毁了这些树，如果浇水，每一棵成活的树的后代会变得越来越娇弱。所以你得把它们的生长环境变得艰苦些，尽早淘汰那些弱不禁风的树。

他还告诉我用水浇灌的树的根是如何的浅，而那些没有浇水的树的根必须钻入深深的泥土获得水分。我将他的话理解为：深根是十分宝贵的。

所以他从不给他的树浇

him to mean that deep roots were to be treasured.

So he never watered his trees. He'd plant an oak and, instead of watering it every morning, he'd beat it with a rolled-up newspaper. Smack! Slap! Pow! I asked him why he did that, and he said it was to get the tree's attention.

Dr. Gibbs went to glory a couple of years after I left home. Every now and again, I walked by his house and looked at the trees that I'd watched him plant some twenty-five years ago. They're **granite** strong now. Big and **robust**. Those trees wake up in the morning and beat their chests and drink their coffee black.

I planted a couple of trees a few years back. Carried water to them for a solid summer. Sprayed them. Prayed over them. The whole nine yards. Two years of coddling has resulted in trees that expect to be waited on hand and foot. Whenever a cold wind blows in, they **tremble** and **chatter** their branches. **Sissy** trees.

Funny things about those trees of Dr. Gibbs'. Adversity and **deprivation** seemed to benefit them in ways comfort and ease never could.

Every night before I go to bed, I check on my two sons. I stand over them and watch their little bodies, the rising and falling of life within. I often pray for

水。他种了一棵橡树，每天早上，他不是给它浇水，而是用一张卷起的报纸抽打它。"啪！噼！砰！"我问他为什么这样做，他说是为了引起树的注意。

在我离家两年后，吉布斯医生就去世了。我常常经过他的房子，看着25年前我曾看着他种下的那些树。如今它们已是像石头般硬朗了。枝繁叶茂、生气勃勃。这些树在早晨醒过来，拍打着胸脯，啜饮着苦难的汁水。

几年前我也种下两三棵树。整整一个夏天我都坚持为它们浇水。为它们喷杀虫剂，为它们祈祷。整整9平方码大的地方。两年的悉心呵护，结果两棵树弱不禁风。每当寒风吹起，它们就颤抖起来，枝叶直打战。娇里娇气的两棵树。

吉布斯医生的树真是有趣。逆境和折磨带给它们的益处似乎是舒适和安逸永远无法给予的。

每天晚上睡觉前，我都要看看两个儿子。我俯视着他们那幼小的身体，生命就在其中起落沉浮。我总是为他们祈祷，总是祈祷他们的生活能一帆风顺。但后来我想是该改变我的祈祷词的时候了。

them. Mostly I pray that their lives will be easy. But lately I've been thinking that it's time to change my prayer.

This change has to do with the **inevitability** of cold winds that hit us at the core. I know my children are going to encounter hardship, and I'm praying they won't be naive. There's always a cold wind blowing somewhere.

So I'm changing my prayer. Because life is tough, whether we want it to be or not. Too many times we pray for ease, but that's a prayer seldom met. What we need to do is pray for roots that reach deep into the Eternal, so when the rains fall and the winds blow, we won't be swept **asunder**.

这改变是因为将吹在我们要害的不可避免的寒风。我知道我的孩子们将遇到困难，我祈祷他们不会太天真幼稚。在某些地方总会有寒风吹过。

所以我改变了我的祈祷词。因为不管我们愿不愿意，生活总是艰难的。我们已祈祷了太多的安逸，但却少有实现。我们所需要做的是祈祷深植我们的信念之根，这样我们就不会被雨打风吹所伤害。

单词解析 Word Analysis

yell [jel] *vt.* & *vi.* 叫喊，大声叫；叫喊着说

例 Something brushed past Bob's face and he let out a yell.
有什么东西从鲍勃的脸上扫过，他大叫了一声。

circumstance ['sɜːkəmstəns] *n.* 环境，境遇；事实，细节

例 Recent opinion polls show that 60 percent favor abortion under certain circumstances.
最近的民意调查显示，60%的人赞成在某些情况下可以堕胎。

husbandry ['hʌzbəndri] *n.* 农业；资源管理，妥善管理

例 They depended on animal husbandry for their livelihood.
他们以畜牧业为生。

horticulture [ˈhɔːtɪkʌltʃə(r)] *n.* 园艺（学）；园艺学家

例 We'll even cover more complex topics such as horticulture and hydroponics gardening.
我们甚至会包括更加复杂的课题，如园艺和无土栽培园艺。

spoil [spɔɪl] *vt.* 损坏，糟蹋；溺爱，宠坏

例 It's important not to let mistakes spoil your life.
重要的是不要让错误毁了你的生活。

successive [səkˈsesɪv] *adj.* 连续的，相继的；继承的，接替的

例 Jackson was the winner for a second successive year.
杰克逊已经是连续第二年获胜了。

weenie [ˈwiːni] *adj.* 微小的，细小的

例 So you have to make things rough for them weed out the weenie trees early on.
所以你得把它们的生长环境变得艰苦些，尽早淘汰那些弱不禁风的树。

shallow [ˈʃæləʊ] *adj.* 浅的，肤浅的；表面的，皮毛的

例 Put the milk in a shallow dish.
将牛奶倒入一个浅盘里。

granite [ˈɡrænɪt] *n.* 花岗石；坚毅，坚韧不拔

例 Some part of project cases of granite floor tile and wall tile.
部分花岗岩地砖和墙砖的工程案例。

robust [rəʊˈbʌst] *adj.* 精力充沛的；坚定的

例 More women than men go to the doctor. Perhaps men are more robust or worry less?
看医生的女性多于男性。也许男性更强壮或者顾虑要少一些？

tremble [ˈtrembl] *vi.* 发抖；颤动；焦虑；轻轻摇晃

例 His mouth became dry, his eyes widened, and he began to tremble all over.
他嘴唇发干，眼睛圆睁，全身开始颤抖起来。

Growing Roots 07
成长的树根

chatter ['tʃætə(r)] *vi.* 振动，打颤；唠叨
- 例 She was so cold her teeth chattered.
  她冻得牙齿咯咯响。

sissy ['sɪsɪ] *adj.* 女人气的，柔弱的
- 例 Far from being sissy, it takes a real man to accept that he is not perfect.
  只有真正的男人才会接受自己并非完美无缺的事实，这绝不是什么女孩子气。

deprivation [ˌdeprɪ'veɪʃn] *n.* 剥夺；丧失；免职；废止
- 例 Millions more suffer from serious sleep deprivation caused by long work hours.
  另外还有数百万人因工作时间过长而睡眠严重不足。

inevitability [ɪnˌevɪtə'bɪlətɪ] *n.* 必然性；不可避免性
- 例 They accept the inevitability of passing feelings.
  他们能够接受这种情绪来临的必然性。

asunder [ə'sʌndə(r)] *adv.* 分开地；分离地；成数部分（或数块）；化为碎片
- 例 Your conscience, conviction, integrity, and loyalties were torn asunder.
  你的良心、信念、正直和忠诚都被扯得粉碎了。

语法知识点 Grammar Points

① **He never yelled at us for playing in his yard.**

本句中 yell at sb. 为固定搭配，表示"对……大呼小叫"。
- 例 "Please don't yell at me." She began to sniffle.
  "请不要对我喊大叫。"她啜泣起来。

② **He never watered his new trees, which flew in the face of conventional wisdom.**

本句中，which 引导的是一个非限定性定语从句，此处不能用 that 替代；in the face of 表示"面对"，与 flow 一起连用后表示"有悖于……"。

例 The government wilted in the face of such powerful pressure.
政府面对如此大的压力,失去了信心。

He said that the decision flew in the face of natural justice.
他说这个决定有悖天理。

③ **Every now and again, I walked by his house and looked at the trees that I'd watched him plant some twenty-five years ago.**

本句中的 that 引导宾语从句,此处 that 可省略;every now and again 表示"有时,时时,偶尔";walk by 表示"在……旁边走过;走过……";look at 表示"看;审视;评判;接受"。

例 You had to put a shilling in the meter every now and again.
你每隔一段时间就得往煤气表里放1个先令。

So the river is clear now and we like to walk by the riverside.
所以,现在河水清澈了。我们也喜欢在河边散步了。

Isn't it fantastic? Just look at that!
这是不是棒极了?看看那个!

④ **But lately I've been thinking that it's time to change my prayer.**

本句中的 have been thinking 为现在完成进行时,表示"一直在想且持续到现在"。对比 have been done 为现在完成时,现在完成进行时有时有延续性,现在完成时往往没有。

例 They have been widening the road.
他们在加宽马路,但尚未完工。

They have widened the road.
他们已经完成加宽马路。

⑤ **What we need to do is pray for roots that reach deep into the Eternal, so when the rains fall and the winds blow, we won't be swept asunder.**

本句中 what 引导主语从句,what 引导部分在整个句子中做主语;that 引导定语从句,先行词 roots 在从句中做主语,that 不可省略;when 引导时间状语从句。

经典名句 Famous Classics

1. The world can be changed by man's endeavor, and that this endeavor can lead to something new and better. No man can sever the bonds that unite him to his society simply by averting his eyes. He must ever be receptive and sensitive to the new; and have sufficient courage and skill to novel facts and to deal with them.
   人经过努力可以改变世界,这种努力可以使人类达到新的、更美好的境界。没有人仅凭闭目、不看社会现实就能割断自己与社会的联系。他必须敏感,随时准备接受新鲜事物;他必须有勇气与能力去面对新的事实,解决新问题。

2. Having a calm smile to face with being disdained indicates kind of confidence.
   被轻蔑的时候能平静地一笑,这是一种自信。

3. I knew that if I failed I wouldn't regret that, but I knew the one thing I might regret is not trying.
   我知道我如果失败了,我不会后悔;但我知道我可能会后悔的是,没有去尝试。

4. Always bear in mind that your own resolution to succeed is more important than any other one thing.
   永远记住,你自己要成功的决心比其他任何一件事都重要。

5. There is no pressure when you are making a dream come true.
   当你在圆梦时,你就不会有压力。

读书笔记

08 Run Out of the Rainy Season of Your Life
跑出人生的雨季

My life suffered a lot in a summer five years ago. My father died of an accident resulted from drinking, leaving my **emaciated** mother and two younger brothers alone. At that time, I was in a senior high school. After my father's funeral, the whole family was in a worse condition than ever. As the eldest son, I had no choice but to quit school and work in a factory.

Life went on without any wonder. I dare not to ask for more, just hoping to bring up two younger brothers. However, that's not an easy thing, for I can't afford their **tuition** even if I work from day to night without stopping, and much worse, I must take my sick mother into account. The present **misery** made me want to have another try, but it seems **impractical**, for I can't lose this job any more.

A **thread** of hope **sparkled** in those gloomy days suddenly. It was a rainy dusk when I put myself in the rain and walked in the street.

Suddenly the rain stopped! To my **bewilderment**, I raised my head, and found that "the sky" was in fact a dark

5年前的夏天，我的人生痛苦不堪。父亲因酗酒死于一场事故，撇下了我瘦弱的母亲和两个弟弟。那时，我正上高中。父亲葬礼后，全家人比以前的状态更加糟糕。作为长子，我别无选择，只好退学，到一家工厂打工。

日子就这样平淡无奇地过着。我不敢再有更多的奢求，只希望把两个弟弟抚养成人。然而，那不是轻而易举的事儿。因为即使我每天从早到晚不停工作，也难以支付他们的学费，更何况我必须考虑多病的母亲……眼前的困境使我想再努力一次，但又好像不切实际，因为我不能再丢掉这份工作。

一线希望突然照亮了那些阴暗的日子。那是一个雨天的黄昏，我置身雨中，走在街上。

雨突然停了，我感到迷惑，就抬起头，发现"天空"其实是一顶深蓝色的伞。随后，我听到一个深沉的声音。"没有伞，为什么不跑？"一位拄着拐杖的独腿中年人对我说。"如果跑，你就不会被淋

Run Out of the Rainy Season of Your Life
跑出人生的雨季

blue umbrella. Then I heard a deep voice. "Why not running without an umbrella?" a middle-aged man with one leg on crutch said to me, "If you run, you would get less **drenched**." I shook my head, but after a second I thought: right, why not running without an umbrella? His words shocked me deeply. Without my father's protection, could I only be a slave to the fate, and my dream in childhood only an **illusion**?

While walking together in the rain, I knew that he was a promoter from the city, and he received an order and paid much time on it. Facing this guy, I had no sympathy but admiration. I took the umbrella from his right hand and he told me that he once had dreamed of being a policeman, but an accident ruined his dream. Though his present work was demanding and did not suit for his leg, every outing was a wonderful start to him. He was glad that he didn't lose heart and still "ran" on the road of life…

It seems that everything is **destined** but not always. **Enlightened** by the man's remarks, I went to a city in the south and became an assurance representative. After two years' "running", I got somewhere and my family turned better gradually. I came back to my senior high school for the dream in my childhood. The year before

得湿透。"我摇摇头,却转念一想:没有伞,为什么不跑呢?他的话普通却深深地震撼了我。没有了父亲的保护,我就只能做命运的奴隶,童年的梦想就只能是幻想吗?

雨中同行时,我知道了他是城里来的推销员,他接到了一份订单,为此花费了很多时间。面对这个人,我没有怜悯,只有钦佩。我默默地从他的右手里接过伞。他告诉我说他曾想做一名警察,但一次意外事故毁灭了他的梦想。尽管现在的工作非常苛刻,不适合他这腿,但每次出门对他来说都是一个奇妙的开始。他很高兴自己没有丧失勇气,仍然"跑"在人生的道路上……

一切都似乎是命中注定,但又不总是那样。那个人的话让我深受启发,我去了南方的一个城市,成了一名保险代理人。通过两年的"奔跑",我取得了一些业绩,家境也渐渐好转。因为童年的梦想,我又回到了高中。前年夏天,我终于考上了大学。

生活就是这样:当你处在人生的雨季时,如果你无法尽快找到防止雨淋的方法,就会被雨水淋透,但如果你决定摆脱,你会发现,雨季并非像你

last summer, I eventually succeeded in my entrance to university.

Life is like this: when you are in rainy days in your life, if you couldn't find a way to prevent you from being drenched earlier, you would have been **overwhelmed** by it, but if you decided to get rid of it, you'll discover that the rainy days last not so long as you imagined.

Everything is so simple: to run without an umbrella! When you run out of the rainy season of your life, there will be bright sky ahead of you.

原来想的那样长。

一切都是那么简单：没有伞，就跑！跑出人生的雨季，你前面就会是一片晴朗的天空。

单词解析 Word Analysis

emaciated [ɪˈmeɪʃieɪtɪd] *adj.* 瘦弱的，憔悴的
- She was emaciated by long illness.
  长期的疾病把她折磨得瘦骨伶仃。

tuition [tjuˈɪʃn] *n.* 学费
- Annual costs, tuition and fees is £6,600.
  每年的花销、学费和各项杂费有6,600英镑。

misery [ˈmɪzəri] *n.* 痛苦；不幸；穷困；悲惨的境遇
- All that money brought nothing but sadness and misery and tragedy.
  那笔钱带来的只有伤心、痛苦和悲剧。

impractical [ɪmˈpræktɪkl] *adj.* 不切实际的；不现实的；无用的
- When stalking subjects, a tripod is impractical.
  跟踪目标时，用三脚架是不切实际的。

Run Out of the Rainy Season of Your Life
跑出人生的雨季 08

thread [θred] *n.* 线；线索；线状物
例 This time I'll do it properly with a needle and thread.
这次，我要用针线将它缝好。

sparkle ['spɑ:kl] *vi.* 闪耀，闪烁；才华横溢
例 The jewels on her fingers sparkled.
她手指上戴的首饰闪闪发光。

bewilderment [bɪ'wɪldəmənt] *n.* 迷惘，困惑，迷乱
例 He shook his head in bewilderment.
他困惑地摇了摇头。

drenched [drentʃd] *adj.* 湿透的；充满的
例 He was drenched with rain.
大雨浇得他全身都湿透了。

illusion [ɪ'lu:ʒn] *n.* 错觉；幻想；假象；错误观念
例 Floor-to-ceiling windows can give the illusion of extra height.
从地板直抵天花板的窗子会给人以高出实际距离的幻觉。

destined ['destɪnd] *adj.* 命中注定的，预定的；去往……的
例 He feels that he was destined to become a musician.
他觉得自己注定会成为一名音乐家。

enlightened [ɪn'laɪtnd] *v.* 启发；开导
例 Listen to both sides and you will be enlightened; heed only one side and you will be benighted.
兼听则明，偏信则暗。

overwhelm [,əʊvə'welm] *vt.* 压倒；淹没；压垮；覆盖
例 He was overwhelmed by a longing for times past.
他一心渴望回到从前。

语法知识点 *Grammar Points*

① I dare not to ask for more, just hoping to bring up two younger brothers.

本句中有固定词组 dare to do，此处 dare 是实意动词；还有 dare do 的用法，这里 dare 为情态动词；bring up 表示"抚养"。

例 I'll fire you if you dare to do so.
你胆敢这么做，我就开除你。

Don't you dare do him the slightest harm!
不准你动他一根毫毛！

His grandmother and his father brought him up.
是他的祖母和父亲把他养大的。

② However, that's not an easy thing, for I can't afford their tuition even if I work from day to night without stopping, and much worse, I must take my sick mother into account.

本句中 even if 引导条件状语从句，表示"即使，尽管"；from day to night 表示"起早贪黑，不分朝夕"；take...into account 表示"考虑到"。

例 You have to let us struggle for ourselves, even if we must die in the process.
你得让我们为自己拼搏，哪怕我们会在这个过程中死去。

A busy work from day to night: daily briefing and sharing session.
交流团工作由早到晚：每天发出简报与晚上的分享会。

His exam results were not very good, but we must take into account his long illness.
他的考试成绩不是很好，但我们必须考虑到他曾经长期生病。

③ To my bewilderment, I raised my head, and found that "the sky" was in fact a dark blue umbrella.

本句中 that 引导宾语从句，此处可省略；to my bewilderment 为固定搭配，表示"令我困惑的是"；in fact 表示"事实上；实际上，其实"。

例 To my complete bewilderment, she said she liked me.
令我完全茫然的是她说她喜欢我。

Run Out of the Rainy Season of Your Life
跑出人生的雨季 08

You have to admit that you are, in fact, in difficulties.
你不得不承认,你事实上是陷入了困境。

④ It seems that everything is destined but not always.

本句中 it seems that... 是常见搭配,it 在句中充当形式主语,that 引导后面的表语从句。

例 It seems that he is an honest man.
看起来他是个老实人。

⑤ Life is like this: when you are in rainy days in your life, if you couldn't find a way to prevent you from being drenched earlier, you would have been overwhelmed by it, but if you decided to get rid of it, you'll discover that the rainy days last not so long as you imagined.

本句比较长,但实际上是由多个从句组合在一起,句中 when 引导时间状语从句,两个 if 引导条件状语从句。prevent sb. (from) doing sth. 表示"阻止某人做某事"。

例 Nothing would prevent him from speaking out against injustice.
什么也阻止不了他反对不公平的演讲。

Her sudden arrival prevented him from going out.
她突然来到,使他不能外出。

be overwhelmed by 表示"受不起,不敢当"。

例 Do not be overwhelmed by your work and activities.
不要被工作和活动征服。

By planning to the end you will not be overwhelmed by circumstances and you will know when to stop.
如果你计划了这些,你就不会被环境因素征服,也知道什么时候应该停止。

get rid of 表示"除掉,去掉"。

例 I began to have a sinking feeling that I was not going to get rid of her.
我开始有一种永远也摆脱不了她的沮丧情绪。

There's corruption, and we're going to get rid of it.
存在贪污腐败现象,我们将予以清除。

经典名句 Famous Classics

1. There are no secrets to success. It is the result of preparation, hard work, and learning from failure.
   成功没有诀窍。它是筹备、苦干以及在失败中汲取教训的结果。

2. Fear not that the life shall come to an end, but rather fear that it shall never have a beginning.
   不要害怕你的生活将要结束,应该担心你的生活永远不会真正开始。

3. The people who get on in this world are the people who get up and look for circumstances they want, and if they cannot find them, make them.
   在这个世界上取得成就的人,都努力去寻找他们想要的机会,如果找不到机会,他们便自己创造机会。

4. To understand the heart and mind of a person, look not at what he has already achieved, but at what he aspires to do.
   想了解一个人的内心世界,不要看他过去的成就,看他向往做什么。

读书笔记

09 The Shadowland of Dreams
美梦难圆

A young person tells me he wants to be a writer. I always encourage such people, but I also explain that there's a big difference between "being a writer" and writing. In most cases these **individuals** are dreaming of wealth and **fame**, not the long hours alone at the **typewriter**. "You've got to want to write, " I say to them, "not want to be a writer."

The reality is that writing is a lonely, private and poor-paying **affair**. For every writer kissed by fortune, there are thousands more whose longing is never **requited**. Even those who succeed often know long periods of **neglect** and poverty. I did.

When I left a 20-year career in the Coast Guard to become a **freelance** writer, I had no **prospects** at all. What I did have was a friend with whom I'd grown up in Henning, Tennessee. George found me my home—a cleaned-out storage room in the Greenwich Village apartment building where he worked as **superintendent**. It didn't even matter that it was cold and had no bathroom. Immediately I bought a used manual typewriter and felt like a

一个年轻人告诉我他想成为一名作家。我总是鼓励这样的人，但我也解释说，"成为作家"和写作之间有很大的区别。这些人大多数只为追逐名利，殊不知打字机前的写作过程是如此漫长而孤独。"你必须渴望写作，"我告诉他们，"而不是渴望成为作家。"

事实上，写作是孤独的、私人的并且低收入的行当。相对于每一个被命运眷顾的作家而言，还有成千上万个在渴望中打拼的写者。即使那些成功的人也很清楚那种长期的被无视和贫穷的生活。至少我是知道的。

当我离开海岸警卫队结束20年的职业生涯，决定成为一名自由撰稿人时，我一点前途感也没有。我所拥有的是和我一起在田纳西州亨宁市长大的发小。乔治帮我找到住的地方，是在格林尼治村公寓大楼里打扫干净的储藏室，他在那里当管理员。尽管"家"里既阴冷又没有浴室，但这并不碍事。我立刻买了一台二手的打字机，觉得自己是一个真正的

genuine writer.

After a year or so, however, I still hadn't received a break and began to doubt myself. It was so hard to sell a story that I barely made enough to eat. But I knew I wanted to write. I had dreamed about it for years. I wasn't going to be one of those people who die wondering, "What if?" I would keep putting my dream to the test—even though it meant living with uncertainty and fear of failure. And I know that I love this lonely, private and poor-paying affair, simply because I want to write. This is the **shadowland** of hope, and anyone with a dream must learn to live there.

作家。

然而一年后，我依然没有突破，我开始怀疑我自己。卖掉一篇短篇小说很难，因此我几乎都无法挣到足够的食物。但是我确定我非常想写作，这是我梦想很多年的事情。我不会成为那些半途而废的人，沉浸在困惑中思索"如果呢？"我要不断地将梦想付诸实际——尽管这意味着不确定和对失败的恐惧。我知道我喜欢这种孤独的、私人的、低薪的事情，而且仅仅是因为我想写作。这是希望的阴影地带，任何有梦想的人都必须学会在那里生活。

单词解析 Word Analysis

individual [ˌɪndɪˈvɪdʒuəl] *adj.* 个人的；个别的；独特的

例 They wait for the group to decide rather than making individual decisions.
他们等待团体做决定而不是各自做出决定。

fame [feɪm] *n.* 名声；名望；传闻；传说

例 At the height of his fame, his every word was valued.
在他声名鼎盛之时，他的每句话都受到重视。

typewriter [ˈtaɪpraɪtə(r)] *n.* 打字机

例 She took the liberty of using your typewriter while you were away.
你不在时，她擅自用你的打字机。

The Shadowland of Dreams 美梦难圆 09

affair [ə'feə(r)] *n.* 事务；事情，事件；个人的事，私事
例 He was rational and consistent in the conduct of his affairs.
他处理私事时头脑清楚，始终如一。

requite [rɪ'kwaɪt] *vt.* 报答；回报；报复；酬谢
例 The example of requite kindness with enmity was fully applied on North American Indians.
而恩将仇报的例子则被充分地应用到了北美印第安人的身上。

neglect [nɪ'glekt] *n.* 怠慢；被忽略的状态
例 There was a slight but perceptible air of neglect.
有一种微弱但可察觉的冷落意味。

freelance ['fri:lɑ:ns] *adj.* 自由职业的；特约的
例 Michael Cross is a freelance journalist.
迈克尔·克罗斯是一名自由新闻记者。

prospect ['prɒspekt] *n.* 前景；期望；眺望处；景象
例 Unfortunately, there is little prospect of seeing these big questions answered.
不幸的是，几乎不可能看到这些重大问题得到回复。

superintendent [,su:pərɪn'tendənt] *n.* 主管；监督人，管理人
例 He was stopped at the airport by an assistant superintendent of police.
他在机场被一名助理警长扣留了。

genuine ['dʒenjuɪn] *adj.* 真正的；坦率的，真诚的
例 There was a risk of genuine refugees being returned to Vietnam.
存在将真正的难民遣返回越南的风险。

shadowland ['ʃædəʊlænd] *n.* 虚幻境界，阴影地带
例 Deep within the shadowland, time has come for us to rise.
深陷在这虚幻的世界中，我们反击的机会来了。

语法知识点 Grammar Points

① In most cases these individuals are dreaming of wealth and fame, not the long hours alone at the typewriter.

本句中 in most cases 表示 "大多数情况下；大凡"；dream of 表示 "梦想；渴望"。

例 Investors can simply pay cash, but this isn't a workable solution in most cases.

投资者可以直接付现金，但这个办法在大多数情况下都不可行。

He had finally accomplished his dream of becoming a pilot.

他最终实现了成为一名飞行员的梦想。

② The reality is that writing is a lonely, private and poor-paying affair.

本句中 that 引导的是一个表语从句，此处 that 不可以省略。that 在引导宾语从句时和引导定语从句时（引导词充当宾语），可以省略。

例 I promise that I will study hard.

我发誓我会努力学习。（此处 that 可省略）

This is the factory that we visited yesterday.

这就是我们昨天参观过的工厂。（此处 that 可省略）

③ It didn't even matter that it was cold and had no bathroom.

本句中 matter 作为动词，意为 "要紧；有关系"；该句中，that 引导的是一个主语从句，it 在句中充当形式主语，为了避免句子头重脚轻。

例 It is known to us all that the earth goes around the sun.

众所周知，地球围绕太阳转。

It is no matter that he didn't phone.

他没打电话没关系。

④ I would keep putting my dream to the test—even though it meant living with uncertainty and fear of failure.

本句中 live with 意为 "忍受；承认"；even though 意为 "哪怕；即使，纵然"。

例 No man can live with Death and know that everything is nothing.

没人能忍受死亡，且知一切都是虚无。

I will have a try even though I should fail.

哪怕失败，我也要试一下。

经典名句 Famous Classics

1. The more you care, the more you have to lose.
   越在意，失去的就越多。

2. Sometimes you need patience in order to find true happiness. It won't come fast and it won't come easy, but it will be worth it.
   很多时候，为了求得真正的幸福，我们需要保持耐心。因为真正的幸福不会很快到来，也不会轻易到来，但它值得等待。

3. Give me a little bit of time, a little bit of patience, a little bit of faith, to show you how much I love you.
   给我一点点时间，一点点耐心，一点点信心，让我证明我有多爱你!

4. It's okay to be afraid of losing the person you really care. But it's not okay if the person doesn't really care of losing you.
   担心失去一个你在乎的人，情有可原；但是，担心失去一个不在乎你的人，没有必要。

5. Anyone can catch your eye but it takes a special person to catch your heart.
   任何人都可能抓住你的眼球，但只有那个特别的人，才能抓住你的心。

6. I know that life isn't a fairytale, and I'm not asking for a happy ending. All I'm asking is a real imperfect love story about you and me.
   我知道，生活不是童话，所以我不求童话般的结局，只希望拥有一个不完美但却真实的爱情故事，故事的主角只有我和你。

7. Just because someone doesn't love you the way you want them to, it doesn't mean they don't love you with all they have.
   爱你的人如果没有按你所希望的方式来爱你，那并不表示他们没有全心全意地爱你。

10 Face Adversity with Smile
笑对逆境

I told my friend Graham that I often cycle two miles from my house to the town centre, but unfortunately there is a big hill on my way. He said, "You mean fortunately." He explained that I should be glad of the exercise that the hill provided.

Problems are there to be faced and **overcome**. We cannot get anything with an easy life. Helen Keller was the first deaf and blind person to gain a University degree. She wrote, "Character cannot be developed in ease and quiet. Only through experiences of **trial** and suffering can the soul be strengthened, vision cleared, **ambition** inspired and success achieved."

One of the main **determinants** of success in life is our attitude towards adversity. We always face hardships, problems, accidents and difficulties in our life. We cannot choose the adversity but we can choose our attitude towards it.

Douglas Bader had both legs broken because of a flying accident in 1931. He was determined to fly again and become one of the flying aces in the Battle of Britain with 22 victories over the Germans. He said, "Don't listen to

我告诉我的朋友格雷厄姆，我经常骑两英里的车从我家到镇中心，但不幸的是途中有一座大山。他说，"你是幸运的。"他解释说，大山提供了锻炼环境，我应该高兴。

问题是要面对和克服的。我们不能在安逸的生活中得到我们想要的。海伦·凯勒是第一个又聋又瞎的获得大学学位的人。她写道："字符不能在舒适和宁静中开发，只有通过试验和痛苦的经历，灵魂才能得到加强，视野才能得到开阔，雄心才能得到启发并取得的成功。"

人生成功的主要决定因素之一是我们对逆境的态度。我们始终面临的困难、问题、事故和我们的生活中的困难。虽然我们不能选择逆境，但是我们可以选择对待它的态度。

道格拉斯因为1931年的飞行事故导致双腿截肢。他决心再飞，并继续成为领先的飞行精英活跃在英国与德国的22个空中战役中。他说："不要听任何人告诉你，你不能做

Face Adversity with Smile 笑对逆境 10

anyone who tells you that you can't do this or that. That's **nonsense**. Make up your mind, you'll never use **crutches** or a stick, then have a go at everything. Go to school; join in all the games you can. Go anywhere you want to. But never, never let them **persuade** you that things are too difficult or impossible."

How can you change your attitude towards the adversity? Try these steps:

Confront the problem. Do not be afraid of it.

Take a **positive** attitude.

Think about how you will feel when you overcome this adversity.

Develop an action plan for how to **tackle** it.

Many of the great people took these kinds of steps to overcome the difficulties they faced. They chose the positive attitude. They took on the challenge. They won.

这个或那个,那是胡说八道。下定决心,你将永远不会因使用拐杖或一根棍子而变得一事无成。去学校,参加所有的比赛。你可以去任何你想去的地方,但绝不要让他们用事情太困难或不可能完成来说服你。"

如何改变面对逆境时的态度?尝试以下步骤:

面对问题。不要害怕它。

采取积极的态度。

想象你克服障碍后的感受。

制订一个解决问题的行动计划。

许多伟人都采取这些步骤,以克服他们所面对的困难。他们采取了积极的态度。他们选择了挑战。他们赢了。

单词解析 Word Analysis

overcome [ˌəʊvəˈkʌm] *v.* 战胜,克服;压倒,制服

例 Molly had fought and overcome her fear of flying.
莫莉已经努力克服了对飞行的恐惧。

trial [ˈtraɪəl] *n.* 试验

例 New evidence showed the police lied at the trial.
新的证据表明警方在审讯时撒了谎。

055

ambition [æmˈbɪʃn] *n.* 抱负；渴望得到的东西；追求的目标；夙愿

例 Even when I was young I never had any ambition.
即使是年轻时，我也从没有什么雄心壮志。

determinants [dɪˈtɜːmɪnənts] *n.* 决定物，决定因素

例 The windows and the views beyond them are major determinants of a room's character.
窗户和窗外的景色是决定一个房间特色的主要因素。

nonsense [ˈnɒnsns] *adj.* 荒谬的；无意义的 *n.* 胡说，废话，谬论

例 Most orthodox doctors however dismiss this as complete nonsense.
但大多数传统的医生认为此说法完全是胡说八道。

crutch [krʌtʃ] *n.* 拐杖；支持物

例 I can walk without the aid of crutches.
我不用拐杖也能自己走。

persuade [pəˈsweɪd] *v.* 说服；劝说；使相信；使信服

例 We're trying to persuade manufacturers to sell them here.
我们正在努力劝说制造商在这里销售。

confront [kənˈfrʌnt] *vt.* 面对；使面对面

例 She was confronted with severe money problems.
她面临严峻的资金问题。

positive [ˈpɒzətɪv] *adj.* 积极的；确实的，肯定的

例 Be positive about your future and get on with living a normal life.
要对自己的未来充满信心，继续过一种正常的生活。

tackle [ˈtækl] *vt.* 着手处理

例 The first reason to tackle these problems is to save children's lives.
果断处理这些问题的首要原因是为了挽救孩子们的生命。

Face Adversity with Smile
笑对逆境

语法知识点 *Grammar Points*

① **Only through experiences of trial and suffering can the soul be strengthened, vision cleared, ambition inspired and success achieved.**

本句是由 only 引导的倒装语序，当"only＋状语"位于句首时，其后习惯上要用部分倒装。其中，only 后的状语可以是副词、介词短语、从句等。

例 Only in this way can we learn English.
只有这样才能学会英语。

Only then did I understand what she meant.
只有到那时我才明白她的意思。

在 only 后做状语的是从句时，从句不用倒装，要部分倒装的是主句。

例 Only when it rains do you feel cool.
只有下雨时才觉得凉爽一点。

Only when he returned home did he realize what had happened.
当他回到家里时，才知道出了什么事。

② **He was determined to fly again and become one of the flying aces in the Battle of Britain with 22 victories over the Germans.**

本句中 be determined to do 表示"下定决心做某事"。

例 If we really want to promote economic development, we shall have to carry out some key projects, and we must be determined to do so, whatever the difficulties are.
真想搞建设，就要搞点骨干项目，没有骨干项目不行。不管怎么困难，也要下决心搞。

To be playing made me happy so I was determined to do my best.
能够比赛让我很高兴，所以我决定要做到最好。

③ **They chose the positive attitude. They took on the challenge. They won.**

本句中 take on 表示"承担，接受"之意。

例 No other organization was able or willing to take on the job.
没有任何别的组织有能力或愿意承担此项工作。

Don't take on more responsibilities than you can handle.
不要承担过多的责任。

经典名句 Famous Classics

1. The value of a man should be seen in what he gives, not by what he has achieved.
   一个人的价值,应该看他贡献了什么,而不应当看他取得了什么。

2. For a man, what he expects is nothing else but a man who can go all out and devote himself to a good cause.
   对一个人来说,所期望的不是别的,而仅仅是他能全力以赴和献身于一种美好事业。

3. The good faith is a clear spring, it will wash away fraud dirty and let every corner of the world be flowing clean.
   诚信是一股清泉,它将洗去欺诈的肮脏,让世界的每一个角落都流淌着洁净。

4. Knowledge cannot be gained only from experience, but only from the comparison between the rational invention and the observed fact.
   知识不能单从经验中得出,而只能从理智的发明同观察到的事实两者比较中得出。

5. The ideals which have lighted my way, and time after time have given me new courage to face life cheerfully have been kindness, beauty and truth.
   照亮我的道路,并且不断地给我新的勇气去愉快地正视生活的理想,是善、美和真。

读书笔记

11 Companionship of Books
以书为伴

A man may usually be known by the books he reads as well as by the company he keeps; for there is a **companionship** of books as well as of men; and one should always live in the best company, whether it be of books or of men.

A good book may be among the best of friends. It is the same today that it always was, and it will never change. It is the most patient and **cheerful** of companions. It does not turn its back upon us in times of adversity or **distress**. It always receives us with the same kindness; amusing and instructing us in youth, and comforting and **consoling** us in age.

Men often discover their **affinity** to each other by the mutual love they have for a book just as two persons sometimes discover a friend by the admiration which both entertain for a third. There is an old **proverb**, "Love me, love my dog." But there is more wisdom in this: "Love me, love my book." The book is a truer and higher bond of union. Men can think, feel, and **sympathize** with each other through their favorite author. They live in him

通常看一个人读些什么书就可知道他的为人，就像看他同什么人交往就可知道他的为人一样，因为有人以人为伴，也有人以书为伴。无论是书友还是朋友，我们都应该以最好的为伴。

好书就像是你最好的朋友。它始终不渝，过去如此，现在如此，将来也永远不变。它是最有耐心，最令人愉悦的伴侣。在我们穷困潦倒、临危遭难时，它也不会抛弃我们，对我们总是一如既往地亲切。在我们年轻时，好书陶冶我们的性情，增长我们的知识；到我们年老时，它又给我们以慰藉和勉励。

人们常常因为喜欢同一本书而结为知己，就像有时两个人因为敬慕同一个人而成为朋友一样。有句古谚说道："爱屋及乌。"其实"爱我及书"这句话蕴涵更多的哲理。书是更为真诚而高尚的情谊纽带。人们可以通过共同喜爱的作家沟通思想，交流感情，彼此息息相通，并与自己喜欢的作家

together, and he in them.

A good book is often the best urn of a life **enshrining** the best that life could think out; for the world of a man's life is, for the most part, but the world of his thoughts. Thus the best books are treasuries of good words, the golden thoughts, which, remembered and **cherished**, become our constant companions and comforters.

Books possess an **essence** of **immortality**. They are by far the most lasting products of human effort. Temples and statues decay, but books survive. Time is of no account with great thoughts, which are as fresh today as when they first passed through their author's minds, ages ago. The only effect of time have been to sift out the bad products; for nothing in literature can long survive but what is really good.

Books introduce us into the best society; they bring us into the presence of the greatest minds that have ever lived. We hear what they said and did; we see them as if they were really alive; we sympathize with them, enjoy with them, **grieve** with them; their experience becomes ours, and we feel as if we were in a measure actors with them in the scenes which they describe.

The great and good do not die, even in this world. Embalmed in books, their

思想相通，情感相融。

好书常如最精美的宝器，珍藏着人生的思想的精华，因为人生的境界主要就在于其思想的境界。因此，最好的书是金玉良言和崇高思想的宝库，这些良言和思想若铭记于心并多加珍视，就会成为我们忠实的伴侣和永恒的慰藉。

书籍具有不朽的本质，是人类努力创造的最为持久的成果。寺庙会倒塌，神像会朽烂，而书却经久长存。对于伟大的思想来说，时间是无关紧要的。多年前初次闪现于作者脑海的伟大思想今日依然清新如故。时间唯一的作用是淘汰不好的作品，因为只有真正的佳作才能经世长存。

书籍介绍我们与最优秀的人为伍，使我们置身于历代伟人巨匠之间，如闻其声，如观其行，如见其人，同他们情感交融，悲喜与共，感同身受。我们觉得自己仿佛在作者所描绘的舞台上和他们一起粉墨登场。

即使在人世间，伟大杰出的人物也永生不死。他们的精神被载入书册，传于四海。书是人生至今仍在聆听的智慧之声，永远充满着活力。

spirits walk abroad. The book is a living voice. It is an intellect to which we still listens.

单词解析 Word Analysis

companionship [kəmˈpænɪənʃɪp] *n.* 伙伴关系；友情，友谊

例 I depended on his companionship and on his judgment.
我信赖他的友情，也相信他的判断。

cheerful [ˈtʃɪəfl] *adj.* 令人愉快的；欢乐的，高兴的

例 They are both very cheerful in spite of their colds.
他们俩虽然感冒了，可都兴高采烈的。

distress [dɪˈstres] *n.* 悲痛；危难，不幸；贫困

例 Jealousy causes distress and painful emotions.
嫉妒会带来忧虑和痛苦。

console [kənˈsəʊl] *vt.* 安慰，慰问

例 He will have to console himself by reading about the success of his compatriots.
他只能读读同胞们成功的故事来安慰自己。

affinity [əˈfɪnəti] *n.* 密切关系，姻亲关系

例 He has a close affinity with the landscape he knew when he was growing up.
他对这片从小就了解的土地有着一种归属感。

proverb [ˈprɒvɜːb] *n.* 谚语，格言

例 An old Arab proverb says, "The enemy of my enemy is my friend".
一句古老的阿拉伯谚语说，"敌人的敌人是朋友。"

sympathize [ˈsɪmpəθaɪz] *vi.* 同情，怜悯；共鸣

例 I must tell you how much I sympathize with you for your loss, Professor.

教授，我对您遭受的损失深表同情。

enshrine [ɪn'ʃraɪn] *vt.* 珍藏，铭记

例 His new relationship with Germany is enshrined in a new non-aggression treaty.
他与德国的新关系受新的互不侵犯条约的保护。

cherish ['tʃerɪʃ] *vt.* 珍爱；爱护

例 The president will cherish the memory of this visit to Ohio.
总统将铭记这次俄亥俄之行。

essence ['esns] *n.* 本质，实质；香精

例 The essence of consultation is to listen to, and take account of, the views of those consulted.
当顾问的精髓就在于倾听并考虑咨询者的观点。

immortality [ˌɪmɔː'tæləti] *n.* 不朽，不朽的声名

例 The flame is a quasi-religious emblem of immortality.
火焰可以算作不朽的宗教象征。

grieve [gri:v] *vt.* 使伤心；使悲伤

例 He's grieving over his dead wife and son.
他因丧妻失子而悲痛不已。

语法知识点 Grammar Points

① **Time is of no account with great thoughts, which are as fresh today as when they first passed through their author's minds, ages ago.**

本句中 which 引导非限定性定语从句；when 引导时间状语从句；be of no account 表示"无足轻重；毫不足道"；pass through 表示"通过；经过；经历；经历并完成"。

> 例 Till then these items are of no account as useful means of hardware for war.
> 只有实证才能说明它可以作为有效的军事武器。
> He was one of the last of the crowd to pass through the barrier.
> 他是那群人里最后一批跨越障碍的。

② **The only effect of time have been to sift out the bad products; for nothing in literature can long survive but what is really good.**

本句中 sift out 表示"筛出"。

> 例 We get a different impression of the economy if we sift out the figures for imports.
> 如果把进口方面的数字滤除掉，我们对经济的印象就会不同。

经典名句 Famous Classics

1. One of the most difficult, the most humble, most humiliated by fate, as long as hope, will fear nothing.
   一个最困苦、最卑贱、最为命运所屈辱的人，只要还抱有希望，便无所畏惧。

2. There is nothing more extraordinary than the power of nature. There is nothing more magical than the nature of nature.
   没有什么比顺其自然更有超凡的力量。没有什么比顺乎本性更具有迷人的魔力。

3. The darkest hour is that before the dawn.
   黎明前的时分是最黑暗的。

4. Anything one man can imagine, other men can make real.
   但凡人能想象到的事物，必定有人能将它实现。

5. To be good at using others' successful model, others successful model can become a guide, so you have the direction to follow.
   要善于套用别人的成功模式，别人的成功模式可成为一种指引，让你有方向可循。

6. Life is just a series of trying to make up your mind.
生活只是由一系列下决心的努力所构成。

7. Goals determine what you are going to be.
目标决定你将成为为什么样的人。

8. All human wisdom is summed up in two words—wait and hope.
人类所有的智慧可以归结为两个词——等待和希望。

9. Courage and resolution are the spirit and soul of virtue.
勇敢和坚决是美德的灵魂。

读书笔记

12 Think Positive Thoughts Every Day
积极看待每一天

If your life feels like it is lacking the power that you want and the **motivation** that you need, sometimes all you have to do is **shift** your point of view.

By training your thoughts to concentrate on the **bright** side of things, you are more likely to have the **incentive** to follow through on your goals. You are less likely to be held back by **negative** ideas that might limit your performance.

Your life can be enhanced, and your happiness enriched, when you choose to change your **perspective**. Don't leave your future to chance, or wait for things to get better **mysteriously** on their own. You must go in the direction of your hopes and **aspirations**. Begin to build your confidence, and work through problems rather than avoid them. Remember that power is not necessarily control over situations, but the ability to deal with whatever comes your way.

Always believe that good things are possible, and remember that mistakes can be lessons that lead to discoveries. Take your fear and **transform** it into trust; learn to rise above anxiety and

如果你觉得心有余力不足，觉得缺乏前进的动力，有时候你只需要改变思维的角度。

试着训练自己的思想朝好的一面看，这样你就会汲取实现目标的动力，而不会因为消极沉沦停滞不前。

一旦变换看问题的角度，你的生活会豁然开朗，幸福和快乐会接踵而来。别交出掌握命运的主动权，也别指望局面会不可思议地好转。你必须与内心希望与热情步调一致。建立自信，敢于与困难短兵相接，而非绕道而行。记住，力量不是驾驭局势的法宝，无坚不摧的能力才是最重要的。

请坚信，美好的降临并非不可能，失误也许是成功的前奏。将惶恐化作信任，学会超越担忧和疑虑。让"诚惶诚恐"的时光变得"富有成效"。不要挥霍浪费精力，将它投到有意义的事情中去。当你下意识品尝生命的欢愉时，美好就会出现。当你积极地看待生活，并以此作为你的日常准则时，你就会找到快乐的真谛。

doubt. Turn your "worry hours" into "productive hours". Take the energy that you have wasted and direct it toward every **worthwhile** effort that you can be involved in. You will see beautiful things happen when you allow yourself to experience the joys of life. You will find happiness when you adopt positive thinking into your daily routine and make it an important part of your world.

单词解析 Word Analysis

motivation [ˌməʊtɪ'veɪʃn] *n.* 动机；动力；诱因

例 The timing of the attack, and its motivations, are unknown.
袭击发生的时间及其动机尚不清楚。

shift [ʃɪft] *v.* 改变

例 Attitudes to mental illness have shifted in recent years.
最近几年对精神病的态度已有所改变。

bright [braɪt] *adj.* 明亮的，鲜亮的

例 She leaned forward, her eyes bright with excitement.
她身体前倾，眼里闪动着兴奋的光芒。

incentive [ɪn'sentɪv] *n.* 动机；诱因；刺激；鼓励

例 There is little or no incentive to adopt such measures.
几乎没有什么激励政策来促使人们采取这些措施。

negative ['neɡətɪv] *adj.* 消极的，否认的

例 The news from overseas is overwhelmingly negative.
来自海外的消息特别不容乐观。

Think Positive Thoughts Every Day
积极看待每一天 12

perspective [pə'spektɪv] *n.* 观点，看法

例 He says the death of his father 18 months ago has given him a new perspective on life.
他说18个月前父亲的去世让他对人生有了新的认识。

mysteriously [mɪ'stɪərɪəslɪ] *adv.* 神秘地；不可思议地

例 The lights mysteriously failed, and we stumbled around in complete darkness.
灯不知怎么地不亮了，我们在一片黑暗中跌跌撞撞地走着。

aspirations [æspɪ'reɪʃnz] *n.* 志向；强烈的愿望

例 This gives expression to the national aspirations for reforms.
这反映了全国要求改革的心声。

transform [træns'fɔːm] *vt.* 变换；改变；改观

例 Your metabolic rate is the speed at which your body transforms food into energy.
新陈代谢率是身体把食物转换为能量的速度。

worthwhile [ˌwɜːθ'waɪl] *adj.* 有价值的；值得做的

例 The President's trip to Washington this week seems to have been worthwhile.
总统本周的华盛顿之行看来是有价值的。

语法知识点 Grammar Points

① **If your life feels like it is lacking the power that you want and the motivation that you need, sometimes all you have to do is shift your point of view.**

本句中 if 引导一个条件状语从句，句中两个 that 引导定语从句，引导词在从句中做宾语成分，that 可以省略；feel like 表示"感觉好像"。

例 Sometimes I feel like I'm living with a stranger.
有时我觉得自己和一个陌生人生活在一起。

② **You are less likely to be held back by negative ideas that might limit your performance.**

本句中 that 引导定语从句，先行词在从句中做主语成分，此处 that 不可省略；hold back 表示"阻碍，阻止"。

例 The administration had several reasons for holding back.
政府因为几个原因而犹豫不决。

③ **Begin to build your confidence, and work through problems rather than avoid them. Remember that power is not necessarily control over situations, but the ability to deal with whatever comes your way.**

本句中 rather than 表示"（要）……而不……，与其……倒不如……"；deal with 表示"处理，解决"。

例 The zoo needed better management rather than more money.
这座动物园需要更好的管理，而不是更多的资金。

The President said the agreement would allow other vital problems to be dealt with.
总统说这项协议将能使其他关键问题得到解决。

④ **Take your fear and transform it into trust; learn to rise above anxiety and doubt.**

本句中有固定搭配 transform ... into... 表示"把……变成……"。

例 That is our first milestone to transform into a company of developing high-tech environmental monitoring system.
这是本公司转型为高科技环境监控系统的第一里程碑。

经典名句 Famous Classics

1. Omelets are not made without breaking of eggs.
鸡蛋不打破，蛋卷做不成。（不甘愿吃苦，则预期效果达不到。）

2. As long as the world shall last there will be wrongs, and if no man objected and no man rebelled, those wrongs would last forever.
只要这个世界存在，就一定会有不对的地方，而如果没有人提出异议，没有人反抗，这些不对的事就会永远存在。

Think Positive Thoughts Every Day
积极看待每一天

3. History has demonstrated that the most notable winners usually encountered heartbreaking obstacles before they triumphed. They won because they refused to become discouraged by their defeats.
历史经验显示，最显著的胜利者通常在成功前会遇到让人心碎的困难，他们胜利因为他们拒绝因失败而丧志。

4. You can avoid reality, but you cannot avoid the consequences of avoiding reality.
你可以逃避现实，但你不能逃避因逃避现实所产生的后果。

读书笔记

13 Learn to Live in Reality
学会生活在现实中

To a large degree, the measure of our peace of mind is **determined** by how much we are able to live on the present moment. **Irrespective** of what happened yesterday or last year, and what may or may not happen tomorrow, the present moment is where you are—always!

Without question, many of us have **mastered** the **neurotic** art of spending much of our lives worrying about variety of things—all at once. We allow past problems and future concerns to **dominate** present moments, so much so that we end up **anxious**, **frustrated**, **depressed**, and hopeless. On the flip side, we also postpone our **gratification**, our stated **priorities**, and our happiness, often **convincing** ourselves that "someday" will be much better than today. Unfortunately, the same mental **dynamics** that tell us to look toward the future will only repeat themselves so that "someday" never actually arrives. John Lennone once said, "Life is what is happening while we are busy making other plans." When we are busy making "other plans", our children are busy growing up, the people we love are

我们内心是否平和在很大程度上是由我们是否生活在现实之中所决定的。不管昨天或去年发生了什么，不管明天可能发生或不发生什么，现实才是你时时刻刻所在之处。

毫无疑问，我们很多人掌握了一种神经兮兮的艺术，即把生活中的大部分时间花在为种种事情担心忧虑上——而且常常是同时忧虑许多事情。

我们听凭过去的麻烦和未来的担心控制我们此时此刻的生活，以至我们整日焦虑不安，萎靡不振，甚至沮丧绝望。而另一方面我们又推迟我们的满足感，推迟我们应优先考虑的事情，推迟我们的幸福感，常常说服自己"有朝一日"会比今天更好。不幸的是，如此告诫我们朝前看的大脑动力只能重复来重复去，以至"有朝一日"不会真的来临。约翰·列侬曾经说过："生活就是当我们忙于制定别的计划时发生的事。"当我们忙于指定种种"别的计划"时，我们的孩子在忙于长大，

Learn to Live in Reality
学会生活在现实中

moving away and dying, our bodies are getting out of shape, and our dreams are slipping away. In short, we miss out on life.

Many people lives as if life is a dress **rehearsal** for some later date. It isn't. In fact, no one has a guarantee that he or she will be here tomorrow. Now is the only time we have, and the only time that we have any control over. When our attention is in the present moment, we push fear from our minds. Fear is the concern over events that might happen in the future — we won't have enough money, our children will get into trouble, we will get old and die, whatever.

To combat fear, the best strategy is to learn to bring your attention back to the present. Mark Twain said, "I have been through some terrible things in life, some of which actually happened." I don't think I can say it any better. Practice keeping your attention on the here and now. Your effort will pay great **dividends**.

我们挚爱的人离去了甚至去世了，我们的体型变样了，而我们的梦想也悄然溜走了。一句话，我们错过了生活。

许多人的生活好像是某个未来日子的彩排。并非如此，事实上，没人能保证他或她明天依旧还在。现在是我们所拥有的唯一时间，现在也是我们能控制的唯一时间。当我们将注意力放在此时此刻时，我们就将恐惧置于脑后。恐惧就是我们担忧某些事情会在未来发生——我们没有足够的钱，我们的孩子会惹上麻烦，我们会变老，会死去，诸如此类。

若要克服恐惧心理，最佳策略是学会将你的注意力拉回此时此刻。马克·吐温说过："我经历过生活中一些可怕的事情，有些的确发生过。"我想我说不出比这更具内涵的话。经常将注意力集中于此情此景，此时此刻，你的努力终会有丰厚的回报。

单词解析 Word Analysis

determine [dɪˈtɜːmɪn] v. （使）下决心，（使）做出决定

例 He determined to receive the job.
他决定接受这个工作。

irrespective [ˌɪrɪˈspektɪv] *adj.* 无关的；不考虑的；不顾的
例 The laws apply to everyone irrespective of race, color or creed.
法律对人人都适用，不分种族、肤色或信仰。

master [ˈmɑːstə] *vt.* 控制；精通；征服
例 Duff soon mastered the skills of radio production.
达夫很快掌握了广播节目制作的技能。

neurotic [njʊəˈrɒtɪk] *adj.* 神经质的；神经过敏的；神经官能症的；极为焦虑的
例 He was almost neurotic about being followed.
他对被跟踪几乎到了神经过敏的程度。

dominate [ˈdɒmɪneɪt] 支配，影响；占有优势；统治
例 As a child he was dominated by his father.
他小时候由父亲主宰一切。

anxious [ˈæŋkʃəs] *adj.* 焦急的；渴望的；令人焦虑的
例 The foreign minister admitted he was still anxious about the situation in the country.
外交部部长承认对于该国的局势，他仍然颇感忧虑。

frustrate [frʌˈstreɪt] *vt.* 挫败；阻挠；使受挫折
例 These questions frustrated me.
这些问题让我沮丧。

depress [dɪˈpres] *vt.* 压下，压低；使沮丧
例 I must admit the state of the country depresses me.
我必须承认国家的现状让我倍感沮丧。

gratification [ˌɡrætɪfɪˈkeɪʃn] *n.* 满足；满意；喜悦；使人满意之事
例 Most men live only for the gratification of it.
许多人正是终生营营，力求填充自己的欲壑。

Learn to Live in Reality
学会生活在现实中 13

priorities [praɪˈɒrəti] *n.* 优先，优先权；（时间，顺序上的）先，前；优先考虑的事

例 Being a parent is her first priority.
做好母亲是她的头等大事。

convince [kənˈvɪns] *vt.* 使相信，说服，使承认

例 Although I soon convinced him of my innocence, I think he still has serious doubts about my sanity.
虽然我很快便让他相信我是清白的，但是我想他仍然非常怀疑我是否神志正常。

dynamics [daɪˈnæmɪks] *n.* 动态；力度；动力学，力学

例 Scientists observe the same dynamics in fluids.
科学家们在液体中观察到了同样的驱动力。

rehearsal [rɪˈhɜːsl] *n.* 排练，排演；彩排，演习；复述，详述

例 The band was scheduled to begin rehearsals for a concert tour.
这支乐队准备开始为巡演排练。

dividend [ˈdɪvɪdend] *n.* 红利，股息，利息，（破产时清算的）分配金

例 The first quarter dividend has been increased by nearly 4 percent.
第一季度的股息增长了近4%。

语法知识点 Grammar Points

① **To a large degree, the measure of our peace of mind is determined by how much we are able to live on the present moment.**

本句中 to a large degree 表示"在很大程度上"。

例 Textbook plays a very important role in teaching and influences the teaching model to a large degree.
教材在教学中处于十分重要的位置，在很大程度上影响着教学模式。

be determined by 表示"由……决定"。

例 The share price will be determined by bidding from institutional investors.

股票价格将由机构投资商的出价决定。

be able to 表示"能够"。

> We hoped that we should be able to do that.
> 我们希望我们能这样做。

② Without question, many of us have mastered the neurotic art of spending much of our lives worrying about variety of things—all at once.

本句中 without question 表示"毫无疑问"。

> I told him that his child would pass the examination without question. But he didn't calculate so.
> 我告诉他他的孩子将毫无疑问会通过考试的,但他不以为然。

spend in（可以省略in）+doing sth. 表示"花费（时间/金钱）做……"。

> He spends 10 minutes in listening to the English every day.
> 他每天花10分钟听英语。

worry about 表示"担忧,烦恼;惦念"。

> Don't worry about me; I'm very well.
> 别为我担心,我很好。

all at once 表示"突然,立即,一下子"。

> All at once I fell into a state of profound melancholy.
> 我立即陷入无限的愁思之中。

③ When we are busy making "other plans", our children are busy growing up, the people we love are moving away and dying, our bodies are getting out of shape, and our dreams are slipping away.

本句中 when 引导的是一个时间状语从句,句子后面部分 the people (that) we love... 是由 that 引导的宾语从句,此处 that 省略。

grow up 表示"成长"。

> Many young rock hounds grow up to be geologists.
> 许许多多爱好收集岩石的少年,长大后成了地质学家。

get out of 表示"（使）离开,（使）去掉,摆脱,从……中得到,由……溢出"。

> I couldn't get out of going to that wedding.
> 我不能逃避出席婚礼。

slip away 表示"溜走"。

例 Time, money and patience all slip away.
时间、金钱和耐心都会悄悄溜走。

经典名句 Famous Classics

1. Don't let someone who doesn't know your value tell you how much you're worth.
   别让那些不懂珍惜你的人来衡量你的价值。

2. Life doesn't just happen to you; you receive everything in your life based on what you've given.
   发生在你身上的一切都不是偶然。你从生活里得到什么，源于你给予了什么。

3. Everything will be OK in the end, if it's not OK, it's not the end.
   所有的事情到最后都会好起来的，如果不够好，说明还没到最后。

4. Sometimes, too much happiness can be frightening, because you know it's going to end.
   有时候，太多的幸福会让人害怕，因为你知道总会结束。

5. A rainbow wouldn't be a rainbow if it lost one of its colors. Don't lose anything about you. You're beautiful in your way.
   若缺了一色，彩虹也不足称其为彩虹。有关自己的一丁点儿都不要舍去。你自有你的美丽。

读书笔记

14 Extend the Miracle
发挥潜力，创造无限

My skills, my mind, my heart, and my body will **stagnate**, rot, and die lest I put them to good use. I have unlimited **potential**. Only a small **portion** of my brain do I employ; only a **paltry** amount of my muscles do I flex. A hundredfold or more can I increase my accomplishments of yesterday and this I will do, beginning today.

Nevermore will I be satisfied with yesterday's accomplishments nor will I **indulge**, anymore, in self-praise for deeds which in reality are too small to even acknowledge. I can **accomplish** far more than I have, and I will, for why should the miracle which produced me end with my birth? Why can I not extend that miracle to my deeds of today?

And I am not on this earth by chance. I am here for a purpose and that purpose is to grow into a mountain, not to shrink to a grain of sand. **Henceforth** will I apply all my efforts to become the highest mountain of all and I will strain my potential until it cries for mercy.

I have been given eyes to see and a mind to think and now I know a great secret of life for I **perceive**, at last, that

我的技艺，我的头脑，我的心灵，我的身体，若不善加利用，都将随着时间的流逝而迟钝，腐朽，甚至死亡。我的潜力无穷无尽，脑力、体能稍加开发，就能超过以往的任何成就。从今天开始，我就要开发潜力。

我不再因昨日的成绩沾沾自喜，不再为微不足道的成绩自吹自擂。我能做的比已经完成的更好。我的出生并非最后一个奇迹，为什么自己不能再创奇迹呢？

我不是随意来到这个世上的，我生来应为高山，而非草芥。从今往后，我要竭尽全力成为群峰之巅，将我的潜能发挥到最大限度。

我有双眼，可以观察；我有头脑，可以思考。现在我已洞悉了一个人生中伟大的奥秘。我发现，一切问题、沮丧、悲伤，都是乔装打扮的机遇之神。我不再被他们的外表所蒙骗，我已睁开双眼，看破了他们的伪装。

Extend the Miracle
发挥潜力，创造无限 **14**

all my problems, **discouragements**, and **heartaches** are, in truth, great opportunities in **disguise**. I will no longer be fooled by the garments they wear for my eyes are open. I will look beyond the cloth and I will not be deceived.

单词解析 Word Analysis

stagnate [stæg'neɪt] *vi.* 停滞，不流动，不发展 *vt.* 停滞不流；（使）不动

> His career had stagnated.
> 他的事业已经陷入停滞。

potential [pə'tenʃl] *adj.* 潜在的，有可能的 *n.* 潜力，潜能

> The boy has great potential.
> 这个男孩非常有潜质。

portion ['pɔːʃn] *n.* 一部分；嫁妆；分得的财产 *vt.* 把……分成份额；分配

> Damage was confined to a small portion of the castle.
> 城堡仅有一小部分受损。

paltry ['pɔːltri] *adj.* 微小的；不重要的；无价值的；可鄙的

> The parents had little interest in paltry domestic concerns.
> 那些家长对家里鸡毛蒜皮的小事没什么兴趣。

indulge [ɪn'dʌldʒ] *vt.* 迁就，纵容；使满足 *vi.* 沉溺；纵容

> Only rarely will she indulge in a glass of wine.
> 她只是偶尔才喝杯红酒，让自己享受一下。

accomplish [ə'kʌmplɪʃ] *vt.* 完成；达到（目的）；走完（路程、距离等）

> We will manage to accomplish the task in time even though it is difficult.
> 纵然任务艰巨，我们也要及时完成。

henceforth [ˌhensˈfɔːθ] *adv.* 从今以后，今后

例 I promise never to get drunk henceforth.
我保证从此以后再不喝醉了。

perceive [pəˈsiːv] *v.* 理解；意识到；察觉，发觉

例 They strangely perceive television as entertainment.
奇怪的是，他们居然将电视看作娱乐。

discouragement [dɪsˈkʌrɪdʒmənt] *n.* 沮丧；劝阻；使人泄气的事物；阻止

例 Uncertainty is a discouragement to investment.
不确定性令投资者裹足不前。

heartaches [ˈhɑːteɪk] *n.* 心痛，悲伤，伤心

例 You must be happy, otherwise I will be heartache.
请你一定要幸福，不然我会心痛。

disguise [dɪsˈɡaɪz] *vt.* 掩盖；化装；隐瞒，掩饰

例 You'll have to travel in disguise.
你只能乔装出行。

语法知识点 Grammar Points

① **Nevermore will I be satisfied with yesterday's accomplishments nor will I indulge, anymore, in self-praise for deeds which in reality are too small to even acknowledge.**

本句中 which 引导的是一个定语从句；be satisfied with 表示"对……满意"。

例 I told myself I would be satisfied with whatever I could get.
我告诉自己，不管得到什么我都会心满意足的。

in reality 表示"实际上，事实上，实则"。

例 He came across as streetwise, but in reality he was not.
他给人的印象是很适应都市生活，但实际上并非如此。

② **I can accomplish far more than I have, and I will, for why should the miracle which produced me end with my birth?**

Extend the Miracle
发挥潜力，创造无限 **14**

本句中which引导定语从句，why引导原因状语从句；far more than 表示"远超，何止"。

例 The benefit is far more than you can imagine.
其好处远比你想象的更多。

③ **Henceforth will I apply all my efforts to become the highest mountain of all and I will strain my potential until it cries for mercy.**

本句中henceforth是副词，位于句首，用全倒装句序，结构：副词放句首+动词+主语；最高级highest用定冠词the修饰。

④ **I have been given eyes to see and a mind to think and now I know a great secret of life for I perceive, at last, that all my problems, discouragements, and heartaches are, in truth, great opportunities in disguise.**

本句中at last 表示"最后，终于"。

例 Look! It's snowing. Winter is here at last.
瞧，下雪了。终于是冬天了。

in truth 表示"实际上，事实上"。

例 In truth, we were both unhappy.
事实上，我们俩都不快乐。

经典名句 Famous Classics

1. Every second brings a fresh beginning, every hour holds a new promise, every night dreams can bring hope, and every day is what we choose to make it.
   每一秒都是一个新的开始，每小时都坚守着一个新承诺，每晚的美梦总能带来希望，每天到底会怎样取决于你的选择。

2. A smooth sea never made a skillful mariner.
   平静的大海决不能造就出熟练的水手。

3. When we first met, I had no idea that you would be so important to me.
   当我们第一次相见，我并没想到你对我如此重要。

4. If you get simple beauty and nought else, you get about the best things God invents.
只要你拥有纯真的美,你就拥有了上帝创造的最好的东西。

5. "Beauty is truth, truth beauty,"—that is all we know on earth, and all we need to know.
"美就是真,真就是美。"——这就是我们在人间知道和应该知道的一切。

6. Believe it or not. There's somebody out there hoping to meet someone just like you.
不管你信不信,有个人正希望能遇到像你这样的人。

7. Ideals are like stars—we never reach them, but like mariners, we chart our course by them.
人之需要理想,犹如水手之需要星辰;星辰虽不可及,但可以指引我们的航程。

8. Faith is the bird that feels the light when the dawn is still dark.
信念是黎明前天尚黑时感到光明的鸟。

读书笔记

15 On Achieving Success
论成功

We cannot travel every path. Success must be won along one line. We must make our business the one life purpose to which every other must be **subordinate**.

I hate a thing done by halves. If it be right, do it **boldly**. If it be wrong, leave it undone.

The men of history were not **perpetually** looking into the mirror to make sure of their own size. Absorbed in their work they did it. They did it so well that the wondering world sees them to be great, and labeled them accordingly.

To live with a high ideal is a successful life. It is not what one does, but what one tries to do, that makes a man strong. "Eternal **vigilance**," it has been said, "is the price of liberty." With equal truth it may be said, "**Unceasing** effort is the price of success." If we do not work with our might, others will; and they will **outstrip** us in the race, and **pluck** the prize from our grasp.

Success grows less and less dependent on luck and chance. Self-distrust is the cause of most of our failures.

The great and indispensable help

我们不可能把每条路都走一遍。必须执着于一条道路才能获得成功。我们必须有一个终生追求的目标，其他的则从属于这个目标。

我痛恨做事半途而废。如果这件事是对的，就大胆勇敢地去做；如果这件事不对，就不要去做。

历史长河中的伟人并不是靠终日观瞻镜中的自己来衡量自身的形象。他们的形象来自对事业全身心的投入与追求。他们是如此的卓越超凡，于是芸芸众生觉得他们很伟大，并因此称他们为伟人。

为崇高的理想而活着是一种成功的生活。使人变强大的，不是这个人做了什么，而是他努力尝试去做什么。有人说过，"恒久的警惕是自由的代价"，那同样也可以说，"不懈的努力是成功的代价"。倘若我们不尽全力工作，别人会尽全力，随后他们将在竞争中超越我们，从我们手中夺取胜利的果实。

成功越来越不依赖于运气和巧合。丧失自信是我们失败

to success is character. Character is a **crystallized** habit, the result of training and **conviction**. Every character is influenced by heredity, environment and education. But these apart, if every man were not to be a great extent the architect of his own character, he would be a **fatalist**, and irresponsible creature of circumstances.

Instead of saying that man is a creature of circumstance, it would be nearer the mark to say that man is the architect of circumstance. From the same materials one man builds palaces, another hovel. Bricks and **mortar** are mortar and bricks, until the architect can make them something else.

The true way to gain much is never to desire to gain too much.

Wise men don't care for what they can't have.

的主要原因。

性格是取得成功不可或缺的重要助力。性格是一种固化成形的习惯,是不断培养并坚信于此的结果。每个人的性格都会受到遗传因素、环境和教育的影响。但除此之外,如果人在很大程度上不能成为自己性格的构筑者,那么他就会沦为宿命论者,从而成为环境的失败造物。

与其说人是环境的造物,不如说人是环境的建筑师更贴切些。同样的材料,有人能用其建造出宫殿,而有人只能建成简陋的小屋。在建筑师将其变成他物之前,砖泥依然是砖泥。

想得到的多就永远不要奢望太多。

智者不会在意他们得不到的东西。

单词解析 Word Analysis

subordinate [sə'bɔːdɪnət] *adj.* 下级的;(级别或职位)较低的;次要的;附属的

例 Haig tended not to seek guidance from subordinates.
黑格不愿向下属请教。

boldly ['bəʊldlɪ] *adv.* 大胆地;显眼地

例 We should boldly give them work and promote them and not be overcautious.

我们要放手地任用和提拔他们,不要畏首畏尾。

perpetually [pəˈpetʃuəli] *adv.* 不断地;永恒地;终身地
- He was perpetually involving himself in this long lawsuit.
  他使自己无休止地卷入这场长时间的诉讼。

vigilance [ˈvɪdʒɪləns] *n.* 警惕;警戒
- Constant vigilance is necessary in order to avoid accidents.
  为了避免意外事故,必须经常保持警惕。

unceasing [ʌnˈsiːsɪŋ] *adj.* 不停的,不断的,持续的
- Human society makes unceasing progress.
  人类社会总是不断进步的。

outstrip [ˌaʊtˈstrɪp] *vt.* 超过,越过;优于,胜于
- In the mid-eighteenth century the production of food far outstripped the rise in population.
  18世纪中叶,食物的产量远远超过人口的增长。

pluck [plʌk] *vt.* 拔掉;采,摘
- He plucked the cigarette from his mouth and tossed it out into the street.
  他从嘴里抽出香烟,把它扔到街上。

crystallized [ˈkrɪstəlaɪzd] *adj.* 结晶的,使晶状的
- You can break through and challenge your crystallized patterns and mind-sets.
  你可以突破和挑战你的固化模式和心态。

conviction [kənˈvɪkʃn] *n.* 定罪;信念;确信;说服
- It is our firm conviction that a step forward has been taken.
  我们坚信已经向前迈进了一步。

fatalist [ˈfeɪtəlɪst] *n.* 宿命论者
- I guess I am a fatalist.
  我猜我是个宿命论者。

mortar ['mɔːtə(r)] *n. 砂浆*

例 The two sides exchanged fire with artillery, mortars and small arms.
双方交火时动用了大炮、迫击炮和轻武器。

语法知识点 Grammar Points

① **To live with a high ideal is a successful life. It is not what one does, but what one tries to do, that makes a man strong.**

本句中 to 引导不定式做主语，相当于一个条件从句。it 做形式主语，后接部分为强调成分，not...but...表示"不是……而是……"，该句型中要注意主谓一致，谓语动词采用就近原则。

例 To build an expressway across the country requires a lot of money.
建一条贯通全国的高速公路需要很多钱。

To see her is to love her.
见了她就会爱上她。

I said (to the G8) we have come here not as petitioners but as partners in a fair management of the global community of nations, he said.
他表示：我曾（向八国集团）表示，我们到这里来，不是作为请愿者，而是作为公平管理国际社会的合作者。

② **Instead of saying that man is a creature of circumstance, it would be nearer the mark to say that man is the architect of circumstance.**

本句中 instead of 为介词短语，它后面可跟名词、代词、动名词、介词短语或形容词等。instead 是副词，表示"代替，顶替"。

例 The economy is shrinking instead of growing.
经济正在萎缩而不是在增长中。

The kitchen might have been workable had Nicola kept it tidy; instead it was littered with pots and pans.
如果妮古拉会收拾，厨房本来是能用的；但现在，这里到处乱放着锅碗瓢盆。

③ **Bricks and mortar are mortar and bricks, until the architect can make them something else.**

本句是由 until 引导的时间状语从句，表示"直到……为止"，until 用作连词引导时间状语从句时，从句表示的如果还没有发生，习惯上也要用一般现在时。

例 Don't leave until we come back.
在我们回来之前，不要离开。

We won't go home until the rain stops.
我们要直到雨停了才回家。

经典名句 Famous Classics

1. The very reputation of being strong-willed, plucky and indefatigable is of priceless value.
   意志坚强、胆量过人和不屈不挠的名声，乃是一种无价之宝。

2. If your ship doesn't come in, swim out to it!
   如果你的船不驶进来，那你就朝它游过去吧！

3. Whenever you have an aim you must sacrifice something of freedom to attain it.
   不论什么时候，只要你有一个目标，就得牺牲一定的自由去实现它。

4. We always have time enough, if we will but use it alright.
   只要我们能善用时间，就永远不愁时间不够用。

5. Have an aim in life, or your energies will all be wasted.
   人生应有目标，否则你的努力将成徒劳。

6. There is no paradise on earth equal to the union of love and innocence.
   人世间最大的幸福莫过于既有爱情又爱得纯洁无瑕。

16 Don't Wait for Life to Start
人生莫待绽放

Many people are **constantly** waiting for their life to start. "When I'm older I'll do this" and "In a few years I'll do that." They think the life they are experiencing is boring and meaningless.

Who has never viewed himself/herself as **worthless** and unattractive?

In others' eyes, you are always "the funny one" and became loud and **overconfident** to mask what I was actually feeling, but few people know about the way you felt.

All of us may suffer with **depression** and **frustration**, lose guidance and support, need aids physically, **emotionally**, or spiritually.

Just think like this way:

"This too shall pass."

Horrible feelings I am feeling will **eventually** go away.

I need to stop feeling so sorry for myself and actually want to change. I am an **incredibly** lucky person who have come from a family who love and support my whole life.

I had to be the one to make the decision to change my way of thinking.

All the good things and all the

很多人都在等待自己生命的新起点，总说"等我长大一点，我会做这个"又或者"几年后，我要做那个"。他们觉得现在的生活很乏味无趣。

谁没有试想自己是毫无价值、毫不吸引人的人？

在别人的眼中，你可能是一个"很有趣的人"。你用大声喧器和过度的自信来掩盖自己真正的想法，以致身边的人都看不透你。

我们所有人都会经历挫折和沮丧，失去指引和支持，无论物质、情感还是精神上都急切需要治愈。

请像这样思考：

"这一切都会过去的。"

所有恐惧不安的思想终有一天会烟消云散。

不应再自怨自艾，而要切切实实地谋求改变。能有一个爱护和支持自己的家庭，你已经是世上非常幸运的人了。

只有你可以决定自己想法的转变。

跟不幸一样，在你生命中所有好的事情、身边很棒的

Don't Wait for Life to Start
人生莫待绽放

wonderful people in my life would pass eventually too. While I am feeling miserable, my life is still going on and I am missing out on appreciating those **precious** moments.

We all have horrible things happen to us that will affect each of us differently.

The important thing to remember is that our problems aren't what define us. What defines us is how we deal with what has happened to us; how we change the way we think about it.

We can either let it become us or we can use our new found wisdom to change the little bit of world around us all.

There's something much bigger than us and our problems. It is always important to remember that there is always someone who is in a position much worse than our own.

Nevertheless, I am well on the way to becoming the person I want to be and I have goals and **expectations** of myself. I am now aware that my life has started.

It started years ago and it's not nearly over yet. It's happening right now. Yours is too.

人，同样会有离你而去的一天。当自己沉溺于痛苦之中，而生命的时间漏斗仍不停流转，那你将错过那些值得赞美的珍贵时刻。

尽管境遇相同，但其对不同的人的影响却不尽相同。

重要的是，你要记住，我们遇到的问题不能定义我们的本质。能定义我们的，是我们处理问题的方法，以及我们对待问题的态度转变。

我们或许放任自流，又或许利用我们发现的新智慧改变我们周边发生的事情。

比我们自身和我们所遇到的问题还重要的事情大有所在。切勿忘记永远有人比我们遭遇的更糟糕。

然而，我们有自己的目标和期待，并在自己选择的人生道路上很好地前进着。我们必须从现在起意识到属于自己的人生其实已经开始。

我的人生在很久之前已经开始了，而且还没结束。现在还是进行时。你的也一样。

我的梦想美文：有梦想谁都了不起

单词解析 Word Analysis

constantly ['kɒnstəntli] *adv.* 不断地，时常地

例 His brainwaves were constantly monitored.
对他的脑电波进行了连续监测。

worthless ['wɜːθləs] *adj.* 无价值的，不值钱的；卑微的；不足道的

例 The guarantee could be worthless if the firm goes out of business.
如果厂家倒闭，保修单就会变得毫无用处。

overconfident [ˌəʊvəˈkɒnfɪdənt] *adj.* 过于自信的，自负的

例 He proved overconfident on the witness stand, misremembering a key piece of evidence.
他在证人席上表现得过于自信，记错了一条重要的证据。

depression [dɪˈpreʃn] *n.* 萎靡不振，沮丧

例 Mr. Thomas was suffering from depression.
托马斯先生患有抑郁症。

frustration [frʌˈstreɪʃn] *n.* 挫折；挫败；失意；失败

例 Frustration, anger and desperation have led to a series of wildcat strikes.
挫败感、愤怒和绝望引起了一系列自发性的罢工。

emotionally [ɪˈməʊʃənəli] *adv.* 感情上，情绪上；冲动地

例 Men go through a change of life emotionally just like women.
男人和女人一样，也要在情绪上经历更年期。

eventually [ɪˈventʃuəli] *adv.* 终究；终于，最后；竟；总归

例 Eventually, the army caught up with him in Latvia.
最终，大部队在拉脱维亚赶上了他。

incredibly [ɪnˈkredəbli] *adv.* 难以置信地，很，极为

例 Being tall can make you feel incredibly self-confident.
个子高会使你感觉极其自信。

Don't Wait for Life to Start
人生莫待绽放 16

precious ['preʃəs] *adj.* 贵重的；宝贵的，珍贵的

例 After four months in foreign parts, every hour at home was precious.
在国外待了4个月后，在家的每一刻都是宝贵的。

nevertheless [,nevəðə'les] *adv.* 不过；然而；仍然；尽管如此

例 Most marriages fail between five and nine years. Nevertheless, people continue to get married.
大部分婚姻在婚后第5~9年间失败，然而，人们仍会选择结婚。

expectations [ekspek'teɪʃnz] *n.* 希望；预料；（被）预期；期望的事情

例 His performance exceeded all expectations.
他的表演超出了所有人的期待。

语法知识点 Grammar Points

① **In others' eyes, you are always "the funny one" and became loud and overconfident to mask what I was actually feeling, but few people know about the way you felt.**

本句中 in other's eyes 表示"在某人的眼里"，为固定短语；类似常见短语还有 in other ways。

例 Sometimes I think, the called happiness just exist in other's eyes, we always think others are very happy and we are poor guys.
有的时候，我觉得所谓的幸福都是别人眼里的，我们总是很容易觉得别人幸福觉得自己可怜。

I think it is time for us to lay down our face, live the way we are, don't live in other's eyes.
我认为是时候该放下我们的面子，活出自我，不要活在别人的眼光里。

② **I am an incredibly lucky person who have come from a family who love and support my whole life.**

本句中两个 who 引导定语从句，第一个who 先行词是 I，第二个 who 先行词是 a family。

③ **While I am feeling miserable, my life is still going on and I am missing out on appreciating those precious moments.**

本句中 while 引导时间状语从句，表示"当……时候"；miss out 表示"遗漏（忘）"。

例 There should be an apostrophe here, and look, you've missed out the word "men" altogether!
这里应该有一个撇号，还有你看，你把men这个单词整个儿漏掉了！

④ **We can either let it become us or we can use our new found wisdom to change the little bit of world around us all.**

本句中 either...or... 表示"要么……要么……"。

例 Most single parents are either divorced or separated.
大多数单身父母要么是离婚的，要么是分居的。

经典名句 Famous Classics

1. The success of the character: brave and honest; challenge life; gentle; generous; helpfulness; courtesy; low-key life; self-reliance.
   成功人的性格：勇敢正直，挑战生活，态度温和，宽厚待人，乐于助人，礼貌谦和，低调做人，自强自立。

2. Every rose has its thorn, and every man's character has something that you can't stand.
   每一枝玫瑰都有刺，正如每个人的性格里都有你不能容忍的部分。

3. There is no desperate situation in the world, only those who are in desperate condition.
   世上没有绝望的处境，只有对处境绝望的人。

4. As fruit needs not only sunshine but cold nights and chilling showers to ripen it, so character needs not only joy but trial and difficulty to mellow it.
   水果不仅需要阳光，也需要凉夜。寒冷的雨水能使其成熟；人的性格陶冶不仅需要欢乐，也需要考验和困难。

5. The length of life is not important, as long as you live happily, do

Don't Wait for Life to Start
人生莫待绽放

something meaningful in your lifetime, then it is enough.
生命之长短并不重要，只要你活得快乐，在有生之年做些有意义的事，便已足够。

6. No matter when you start, it is important that you do not stop after starting. No matter when you end, it is important that you do not regret after the end.
不管从什么时候开始，重要的是开始以后不要停止；不管在什么时候结束，重要的是结束以后不要后悔。

7. Experience without learning is better than learning without experience.
有经验而无学问胜于有学问而无经验。

8. Hope is itself a species of happiness, and perhaps the chief happiness which this world affords.
希望本身就是一种幸福，也许还是这个世界提供给我们的最大幸福。

读书笔记

17 Never Too Late to Become What You Want to Be
梦想终有成真时

The first day of school our professor introduced a little old lady to us. "Why are you in college at such a young age?" I asked later. She jokingly replied, "I'm here to meet a rich husband, get married, have a couple of children, and then retire and travel." "No, seriously," I asked. I was curious what may have **motivated** her to be taking on this challenge at her age. "I always dreamed of having a college education and now I'm getting one!" she told me. We became **instant** friends.

Every day for the next three months we would leave class together and talk nonstop. I was always listening to this "time machine" as she shared her wisdom and experience with me. At the end of the semester we invited Rose to make a speech to our football team. I'll never forget what she taught us. As she began to **deliver** her prepared speech, she dropped her note card on the floor. A little embarrassed, she simply said, "I'm sorry. This whiskey is killing me! I'll never get my speech back in order, so let me just tell you what I know." As we laughed, she cleared her throat and

在开学的第一天，我们的老师向我们介绍了一位小老太太同学。之后我问那位老太太："为什么你这么年轻还来上大学呢？"她开玩笑地回答道："我来这是想找一个有钱的老公，结婚生子，然后退休，去旅游。"我又说："我是认真的，不开玩笑。"我非常好奇，是什么激励她在这个年纪还要接受这份挑战。她告诉我："我一直梦想接受大学教育，现在我就得到啦！"从那之后，我们成了朋友。

接下来的三个月里我们每天都一起离开教室，不停地聊天。我非常喜欢听这位"时光机"跟我分享她的智慧和经验。学期末我们邀请她给足球队做演讲。我永远不会忘记她教给我们的东西。当她开始发表准备好的演讲时，她的稿子掉到了地上。带着一丝尴尬，她简洁地说道："不好意思，威士忌太烈了，把我弄得晕头转向的。我没法把我的演讲稿重新排列了，所以就让我跟你们说说我知道的事情吧。"在

Never Too Late to Become What You Want to Be
梦想终有成真时

began: "We do not stop playing because we are old; we grow old because we stop playing. There are only two secrets to stay young, being happy and achieving success. You have to laugh and find humor every day. You've got to have a dream. When you lose your dreams, you die. We have so many people walking around who are dead and don't even know it! There is a huge difference between growing older and growing up. If you are nineteen years old and lie in bed for one full year and don't do one **productive** thing, you will turn twenty years old. Anybody can grow older. That doesn't take any talent or ability. The idea is to grow up by always finding the opportunity in change. Have no regrets. The **elderly** usually don't have regrets for what we did, but rather for things we did not do. The only people who fear death are those with regrets."

At the year's end Rose finished the college degree. One week after graduation Rose died **peacefully** in her sleep. Over two thousand college students attended her funeral to honor the wonderful woman who taught by example that it's never too late to be all you can possibly be.

我们大笑的时候她清了清嗓子，开始演讲："我们不会因为年龄的增长而放弃追逐梦想；当我们放弃的时候我们才是真的变老了。保持年轻有两个秘诀：一是变得快乐，二是向成功的方向努力。每一天你都需要开开心心的。你也必须要有梦想。当你连梦想都丢弃的时候，人生就失去了意义。我们身边有很多人每天行尸走肉地活着，甚至他们自己都没有意识到！年龄增长和长大有很大的不同。如果你现在十九岁，躺在床上一整年，一件有用的事情都不做，你还是会进入二十岁。每个人的年龄都会增长。这不需要任何天赋或能力。而总是寻求改变的机会的人才会真正长大。他们毫无遗憾。年长的人通常不会因为做过的事情，而会因为那些没做的事情感到遗憾。唯一害怕死亡的人都是那些留有遗憾的人。"

年底她拿到了大学学位。毕业后一周，她在睡梦中平静地去世了。两千多名大学生参加了她的葬礼，共同纪念这个伟大的女人，她用自身做例子教会我们，梦想终有成真时。

我的梦想美文：有梦想谁都了不起

单词解析 Word Analysis

motivate ['moutɪveɪt] *v.* 激发（兴趣或欲望）；给予动机

例 A good teacher is one who can motivate his students.
好老师是能激励学生的老师。

instant ['ɪnstənt] *adj.* 立即的；即时的；速成的

例 Just for an instant I thought he was going to refuse.
我脑中有一闪念，以为他要拒绝了。

deliver [dɪ'lɪvər] *v.* 递送；发表（演讲）；交付；接生；履行

例 The mailman delivers letters and parcels every morning.
邮差每天早晨递送信件和包裹。

productive [prə'dʌktɪv] *adj.* 生产的；有成效的；多产的

例 Their productive cycle covers several decades.
它们的生产周期可延续几十年。

elderly ['eldərli] *adj.* 年老的；年长的

例 Many elderly people live an idle life.
许多老年人过着悠闲的生活。

peacefully ['pi:sfəli] *adv.* 平静地；和平地

例 The old man dropped off peacefully in his sleep.
老人在睡眠中平静地死去。

语法知识点 Grammar points

① **I was curious what may have motivated her to be taking on this challenge at her age.**

这个句子是 what 引导的宾语从句，what 在从句中做主语。

例 I felt curious how that guy would head for such a miserable end.
我感到奇怪，那家伙怎么会落得这样一个可悲的结局。

may have done 是指"某事可能已经做了"，表示对过去的一种推测。

Never Too Late to Become What You Want to Be
梦想终有成真时

> He may have done that math question before.
> 他以前可能做过那道数学题。

take on 承担；呈现；接受；从事；较量；开始雇用

> We can't take on any more work, and we're fully stretched at the moment.
> 我们不能再接受更多的工作了，目前已经全力以赴了。
>
> Then your company must take on a new look now.
> 那你们公司现在肯定呈现出一番新的面貌了。

take 有很多固定搭配。如：take away 拿开，拿走；减去；剥夺；夺取；抢夺。take down 取下；拿下；拆卸；记录；记下。take in 欺骗；使上当；领会；理解；接待；收留；吸入。take off 拿走，取下；脱去；截断，切除；起跳；起飞。take over 接管；接替。

② I was always listening to this "time machine" as she shared her wisdom and experience with me.

这个句子中always与进行时连用，表示喜欢或者厌恶，带有感情色彩。as引导的是时间状语从句，这时as用作连词。

> A sudden chill of horror swept over her as she felt the drip of saliva upon her hand.
> 当她感觉到滴到她双手上的唾液时，恐怖的寒慄突然遍布了她全身。

share sth. with sb. 与某人分享某物

> Keep your fears to yourself, but share your courage with others.
> 把恐惧留给自己，和他人分享勇气。

③ The elderly usually don't have regrets for what we did, but rather for things we did not do.

这个句子中，what引导的是宾语从句，what在从句中做宾语。

> I can't remember what you told me.
> 我忘了你跟我说的话了。

have regrets for 的意思是"对……感到后悔"。

> She showed much regret for her fault.
> 她对她的过失深感后悔。

but rather是固定搭配，表示"而宁可说是，反而"。

> 例 He has a strong body, but rather thin legs.
> 他躯干粗壮，但腿却很瘦。

经典名句 Famous Classics

1. We choose our friends by instinct, but we keep them by judgement.
   我们选择朋友靠的是本能，而保持友谊靠的是判断。

2. Love should be based on the premise of ecstasy, and the object seek happiness for their love.
   爱情应该是以忘我为前提的，并要为自己所爱的对象谋求幸福。

3. God created man and, finding him not sufficiently alone, gave him a companion to make him feel his solitude more keenly.
   上帝创造了人类，之后发现他不够孤独，于是给了他一个伴侣好让他更强烈地感受到孤单。

4. Women have served all these centuries as looking-glasses possessing the magic and delicious power of reflecting the figure of a man at twice its natural size.
   几个世纪以来，女人们一直在充当一面能够将男人的形象放大一倍的魔法镜子。

5. Take my word for it, the silliest woman can manage a clever man; but it takes a very clever woman to manage a fool.
   听取我的话，最笨的女人也可以管得住一个聪明的男人；但是要管得住愚蠢的男人，得要一个非常聪明的女人。

6. In her first passion woman loves her lover; in all the others all she loves is love.
   在最初的激情时，女人们爱的是他们的爱人，而其他时候，她们爱的是爱情本身。

7. Experience shows us that love is not looking into one another's eyes but looking together in the same direction.
   经验告诉我们，爱情不是互相注视着对方，而是一起注视着同一个方向。

8. May I be looking at you when my last hour has come, and as I die may I hold you with my weakening hand.
让我在生命走到尽头时看着你，让我在死去的时候用衰弱的手握住你。

9. I always say that if you want a speech made you should ask a man, but if you want something done you should ask a woman.
我常说，如果你想要做一次演说，你应该咨询一个男人；但如果你想真正去完成一件事，你应该去问一个女人。

10. For a crowd is not company; and faces are but a gallery of pictures; and talk but a tinkling cymbal, where there is no love.
众人并非良伴；如果没有爱意，人们的脸孔不过是美术馆中的画作，他们的谈话不过是铙钹的叮当作响。

读书笔记

18 Tiny Steps, Big Changes
寻求大改变，从小处做起

If you have failed in the past at trying to make big changes in your life, try again now, one tiny step at a time. Every year it's the same. As December comes to an end, you think about the New Year and all the ways you want to improve your life. But as you start to write down your hopes for the New Year, you think about last year. You excitedly wrote down all the changes you were going to make, but by the end of January those ideas got lost in your crowded life.

Here's a suggestion: Forget the **overreaching,** hard-to-achieve goals. Just think small. "We have this extreme-makeover culture that thinks you've got to do everything in big steps, even though the evidence is overwhelming that it doesn't work," says psychologist Robert Maurer, who recently published *One Small Step Can Change Your Life*.

"What we try to do is to break down to a step so small that people couldn't possibly resist or have any excuse not to do it." The technique is called "kaizen", a Japanese word for an American business philosophy adapted to change behavior

如果在过去的日子里，你曾寻求人生中的大改变却以失败告终，现在再尝试一次，每次只改变一小处。每年都是一样的。当十二月结束的时候，你考虑着新年的事情，自始至终你都想改变你的生活。当你开始写下新年愿望时，你思考着过去的一年。你兴奋地写下你将要做出的所有改变，但是一月末的时候那些想法却迷失在忙碌的生活里。

这儿有一条建议：忘记不自量力的、很难实现的目标，考虑一些小目标就好了。最近刚出版了《小事改变人生》一书的心理学家罗伯特·莫伊雷尔说："我们有这种彻底改变的文化思想，让你觉得就算不可能实现的证据是压倒性的，也必须要大步地去做每一件事。"

"我们尝试做的就是把步伐减小到人们不会抵制，不会有借口去逃避。"这项技术叫作kaizen，一个日语单词，是用来改变人行为和态度的美国经营哲学。在"二战"期间，美国的工厂经理通过努力实

Tiny Steps, Big Changes
寻求大改变,从小处做起

and attitudes. During World War II, American factory managers increased **productivity** by trying small, continuous improvements rather than sudden **radical** change. After the war, U. S. **occupation** forces brought that philosophy to a rebuilding Japan, which made it a **cornerstone** of the country's amazing economic **rebound**. The Japanese called it kaizen, which means "improvement". Maurer, who teaches at the UCLA and University of Washington Medical Schools, says he began studying whether the idea could help people who couldn't **tackle** big challenges. "Some of it is psychological, and some of it is just their overwhelmed lifestyles," he says, "They don't have the time to go to the gym and do all those other things we know are good for them. So kaizen seemed a logical thing to experiment with."

现小的连续的提高而不是突然的很大的改变来增加了产量。战后,美军把这门哲学带到了重建的日本,成为日本惊人的经济复兴的奠基石。日本人把它叫作kaizen,意思就是"改善"。在加利福尼亚大学洛杉矶分校和华盛顿医学院教书的莫伊雷尔开始研究这些思想是否能够帮助那些不能处理大改变的人。他说:"其中有一些是涉及心理学的,有一些只是他们片面的生活方式。他们没有时间去健身房,没有时间做那些对他们有益的事情。所以就这些方面来说kaizen看起来非常合理。"

单词解析 Word Analysis

overreach [ˌoʊvərˈriːtʃ] v. 做事过头;(靠狡诈)取胜;(伸得过长而)超出;夸大;行骗

> 例 Don't apply for that job. You're in danger of overreaching yourself.
> 不要申请那份工作,以免有不自量力之嫌。

productivity [ˌprɑːdʌkˈtɪvəti] n. 生产率;生产力

> 例 We should aim with efforts for higher productivity.
> 我们应该力争达到更高的生产率。

radical ['rædɪkl] *adj.* 激进的；彻底的；基本的

例 I know you are radical in your thinking, but don't go too far.
我知道你思想激进，但不要走得太远。

occupation [ˌɑːkjuˈpeɪʃn] *n.* 职业；占有；消遣；居住

例 I haven't entered your name and occupation yet.
我尚未记下你的名字和职业。

cornerstone ['kɔːrnərstoʊn] *n.* 隅石；奠基石

例 Indeed, it has come to be the cornerstone of modern thinking on international trade.
事实上，它已成为现代国际贸易理论的奠基石。

rebound [rɪˈbaʊnd] *n.* 篮板球；弹回

例 There was a scramble for the rebound.
球反弹回来后，双方都疯狂地抢球。

tackle ['tækl] *v.* 处理；对付；阻截（对方球员）；与……交涉

例 Can you suggest how we might tackle the problem?
我们怎样处理这问题，你能给出个主意吗？

语法知识点 Grammar points

① As December comes to an end, you think about the New Year and all the ways you want to improve your life.

这个句子有一个as引导的时间状语从句。

例 But as you start to write down your hopes for the New Year, you think about last year.
当你开始写下新年愿望时，你思考着过去的一年。

as用作连词时，可以引导多种从句。

1. 引导时间状语从句

例 Helen heard the story as she washed.
海伦洗衣服的时候听了这个故事。

As I left the house, I remembered the key.
当我离开房间的时候，我想起了钥匙。

The boy's eyes had slowly moved to him as he had spoken.
他说完时，这孩子的眼光慢慢地移到他身上。

2. 引导原因状语从句

> 例 As rain has fallen, the air is cooler.
> 由于下了雨，空气比较凉爽。
>
> I can't come tonight, as I'm going to a concert.
> 今晚我不能来，因为我要去听音乐会。

3. 引导让步状语从句

> 例 Coward as he was, however, Flashman couldn't swallow such an insult as this.
> 弗拉西曼虽然是个胆小鬼，也不能忍受这种屈辱。
>
> Simple as was the idea, the then scientific world would have none of it.
> 虽然这概念很简单，但当时的科学界却不知道这一点。

4. 引导比较状语从句

> 例 Run as fast as you can.
> 你能跑多快就跑多快。

5. 引导方式状语从句

> 例 When in Rome, do as the Romans do.
> 入乡随俗。
>
> Balloons float in the air as boats float on water.
> 气球飘在空中如同船浮在水上一样。

as还可以用作介词，意思是"作为"。

> 例 As a child he lived in Japan.
> 他小的时候住在日本。
>
> He worked as a cashier in a bank.
> 他在一家银行干过出纳。

come to an end 结束

> 例 The meeting came to an end at last.
> 会议终于结束了。

all the ways 一直；一路上；自始至终；感激不尽

> 例 Brainstorm all the ways your visitor would think of your product.
> 绞尽脑汁地想出访问者对你的产品所可能有的一切想法。

② **We have this extreme-makeover culture that thinks you've got to do everything in big steps, even though the evidence is overwhelming that it doesn't work.**

这个句子中有一个that引导的定语从句，先行词是culture，that在从句中做主语；还有一个even though引导的让步状语从句，在这个让步状语从句中还有一个同位语从句，先行词是the evidence，that引导的从句是对the evidence的解释说明，that在从句中不充当任何成分。

③ **After the war, U. S. occupation forces brought that philosophy to a rebuilding Japan, which made it a cornerstone of the country's amazing economic rebound.**

这个句子中有一个which引导的非限制性定语从句，注意which前面有逗号，which指代的前面一句话，which在从句中做主语。

经典名句 Famous Classics

1. The family is the association established by nature for the supply of man's everyday wants.
   家庭是自然建立起来来满足人们的日常需要的组织。

2. Let early education be a sort of amusement; you will then be better able to discover the child's natural bent.
   让早期教育成为一种娱乐吧，这样你会更容易发现孩子的爱好。

3. Children have to be educated, but they have also to be left to educate themselves.
   我们要教育孩子，但也要让孩子们自我教育。

4. It is not only what we have inherited from our fathers that exists again in us, but all sorts of old dead ideas and old dead beliefs and things of that kind and we can never be rid of them.
   我们身上再现的东西并非只有从父辈继承来的财物，还有各种旧的思想、旧的信仰等，我们永远也摆脱不掉它们。

5. If you bungle raising your children I don't think whatever else you do well matters very much.
   如果你没能教育好孩子的话，做别的什么事也都不重要了。

6. The worst families are those in which the members never really speak their minds to one another, they maintain an atmosphere of unreality, and everyone always lives in an atmosphere of suppressed ill-feeling.
最糟糕的家庭是那些不交流的家庭，他们保持着一种脱离现实的氛围，让每个成员都生活在压抑的病态当中。

7. A wise parent humors the desire for independent action, so as to become the friend and adviser when his absolute rule shall cease.
聪明的父母会迁就孩子们渴望独立的心情，这样，当他们无权约束孩子之后，就会变成孩子们的朋友与顾问。

8. Parentage is a very important profession, but no test of fitness for it is ever imposed in the interest of the children.
亲子关系是非常重要的领域，但是却无法在事前检验它是否有利于孩子的成长。

9. The parent who could see his boy as he really is, would shake his head and say: "Willie is no good; I'll sell him."
看清了孩子们的真面目的父母就会摇晃着孩子的脑袋，然后说："威利看上去不太妙，我得把他卖了。"

10. If there were no schools to take the children away from home part of the time, the insane asylums would be filled with mothers.
如果没有学校让孩子们能离开家里一段时间，疯人院里大概会有母亲。

11. Son, brother, father, lover, friend. There is room in the heart for all the affections, as there is room in heaven for all the stars.
儿子，兄弟，父亲，爱人，朋友。人们心里有容纳这么多感情的空间，就像天空中有容纳所有星辰的空间一样。

12. All wars are civil wars, because all men are brothers.
所有的战争都是内战，因为一切人类皆兄弟。

19 Change Your Bad Habit to Good—Modify Your Environment
改掉坏毛病，养成好习惯——改善周边环境

To get yourself started in a new direction, try the Three M's. Three deserve special mention: they're powerful, simple and easy to learn. What's more, individuals who have made successful changes in their lives—changes in eating habits, exercise **regimens**, career paths, coping strategies, and so on—often relied on one or more of these methods. One of the three M's is modify your environment.

People who have never tried this are **astounded** by the **enormous** effect it often has. One of my students got herself bicycling every day simply by putting her bicycle in her doorway before she left for school. When she returned home, that was the first thing she saw, and that's all she needed to start **pedaling** away. I've known several people who have overcome **nail-biting** simply by buying 50 nail files and distributing them everywhere: in their pockets, their desks and their bedrooms. With a nail file always within reach, they tended to groom rather than bite.

My children have used this simple **technique** many times. Justin,

要想开辟人生新道路，试试三个"M"。有三种方法值得特别提及：它们效力强大而又简单易学。此外，那些已成功改变了人生道路的人们，也常常是依靠这些方法中的一种或多种来改变其饮食习惯、养生之道、事业方向和处世策略等。改善周边环境就是其中一个"M"。

从未尝试改善环境的人通常会对所产生的显著效果感到惊奇不已。我的一个学生为了促使自己每天骑车锻炼，采取了离家上学前将自行车放在门道里的简单方法。这样一回家，她首先看见的就是那辆车，而所需做的就是骑上自行车锻炼去。我认识几个人，他们为了改掉咬指甲的坏习惯而买了50把指甲挫并把它们分放到各处：口袋里，书桌上，卧室内。由于指甲挫总能伸手可及，他们就会去修指甲，而不啃指甲了。

我的孩子们多次运用过这样的简单技巧。我17岁的儿子贾斯廷经常把小小的荧光

Change Your Bad Habit to Good—Modify Your Environment

my 17-year-old, often places small **fluorescent** reminder notes at eye level on the inside of the frame of his bedroom door. A recent one read "Remember to shampoo the dog on Saturday or Dad will kill you". (Here he was using exaggeration to good effect.)

The power of rearranging one's space has been well demonstrated in studies since it was first reported in the 1960s. **Psychologist** Israel Goldiamond of the University of Chicago taught this technique to patients with a variety of personal problems. For example, a young woman who had difficulty studying made dramatic strides when she got a better desk lamp and moved her desk away from her bed.

Psychologist Richard Stuart, who **ultimately** became a director at Weight Watchers International, showed in the 1960s that overweight women could lose pounds by modifying both their eating behavior and "**stimulus** environment"—for example, eating from smaller plates and **confining** all food to the kitchen. To change yourself, change your world.

纸记事便条放在他卧室门框内侧齐眼高的位置。前不久的一张上写道："记着星期六给狗洗澡，否则爸爸会杀了你的。"（为了达到良好效果，他这里用的是夸张手法。）

重新布置自己的空间具有很大的影响力，该观点首次提出于20世纪60年代，在诸多研究中已得到充分证明。当时，芝加哥大学的心理学家伊斯雷尔·戈戴蒙德将这一技巧传授给那些为形形色色的私人问题所困扰的病人。就拿一位年轻女士来说吧，她在学习上困难重重，自从换了一个好点儿的台灯并把书桌搬离开床边后，她在学习上就取得了长足进步。

心理学家理查德·斯图尔特最终当上了国际体重观察员组织的总监，他在20世纪60年代曾指出：体重过重的妇女可以通过纠正饮食习惯和改变"刺激食欲的环境"的方法来减肥——例如，用小一点的盘子吃饭和把食物全都集中放在厨房里。要改变自我就必须改变你周围的世界。

单词解析 Word Analysis

regimen ['redʒəmənz] *n.* 生活规则；养生法

例 Whatever regimen has been prescribed should be rigorously followed.
不管制订的是什么样的养生计划，都要严格遵守。

astound [ə'staʊnd] *v.* 使震惊，使大吃一惊

例 He used to astound his friends with feats of physical endurance.
过去，他表现出来的惊人耐力常让朋友们大吃一惊。

enormous [ɪ'nɔːməs] *adj.* 巨大的；庞大的；极恶的；凶暴的

例 There is, of course, an enormous amount to see.
当然有很多可看的。

pedal ['pedl] *v.* 踩自行车的踏板；骑自行车

例 She was too tired to pedal back.
她太累了，没力气骑自行车回去。

nail-biting *n.* 咬指甲癖性；束手无策

例 It's been a nail-biting couple of weeks waiting for my results.
这两个星期等结果，弄得我坐卧不安。

technique [tek'niːk] *n.* 技巧；技能；技术；技艺

例 He went off to the Amsterdam Academy to improve his technique.
他动身前往阿姆斯特丹学院去进修技艺。

fluorescent [ˌflɔː'resnt] *adj.* 荧光的；发荧光的；（颜色、材料等）强烈反光的；发亮的

例 It was lit by hooded fluorescent lamps.
照明用的是带灯罩的日光灯。

psychologist [saɪ'kɒlədʒɪst] *n.* 心理学研究者，心理学家

例 Psychologists tested a group of six-year-olds with a video.
心理学家用一段录像对一组6岁的儿童进行了测试。

Change Your Bad Habit to Good—Modify Your Environment
改掉坏毛病，养成好习惯——改善周边环境 19

ultimately ['ʌltɪmətli] *adv.* 最后，最终；基本上；根本

例 Ultimately, we can change the shape of people's lives.
最终，我们可以改变人们的生活状况。

stimulus ['stɪmjələs] *n.* 刺激物；刺激因素

例 Interest rates could fall soon and be a stimulus to the US economy.
利率可能很快就会下调，从而刺激美国经济。

confine [kən'faɪn] *v.* 限制；局限于；禁闭；管制

例 He did not confine himself to the one language.
他没把自己局限于这一门语言。

语法知识点 Grammar points

① What's more, individuals who have made successful changes in their lives—changes in eating habits, exercise regimens, career paths, coping strategies, and so on—often relied on one or more of these methods.

what's more 此外

例 I don't like pubs. They're noisy, smelly, and what's more, expensive.
我不喜欢酒吧。那里又吵，气味又难闻，更重要的是，花费太多。

You should remember it, and what's more, you should get it right.
你应该记住它，更重要的是，应该正确理解它。

They are going to get married, and what's more they are setting up in business together.
他们就要结婚了，而且还要一起做生意呢。

rely on 信赖，依赖，相当于depend on

例 You can rely on me for help.
你可指望我来帮忙。

② With a nail file always within reach, they tended to groom rather than bite.

with a nail file always within reach 是with复合结构用法，with+宾语+介词短语。

例 With so many strange faces around her, the baby started to cry.
看到周围这么多陌生的面孔，婴儿开始哭起来了。

The girl appeared again, now with a little boy on her back.
那女孩又来了，这次肩上背了个小婴孩。

③ **The power of rearranging one's space has been well demonstrated in studies since it was first reported in the 1960s.**

since表示"自从"时，不管它是用作介词、连词还是副词，它通常都要与现在完成时连用。

例 The works have been closed since January.
一月份以来这些厂就关闭了。

He's put on a lot of weight since he gave up smoking.
他戒烟后体重增加了许多。

④ **For example, a young woman who had difficulty studying made dramatic strides when she got a better desk lamp and moved her desk away from her bed.**

have difficulty (in) doing sth. 做某事有困难

例 Everyone in the town knew him; so we had no difficulty(in) finding his house。
镇上所有的人都认识他，所有我们毫不费力就找到了他的家。

There was much difficulty (in) finding him.
好不容易才找到他。

经典名句 Famous Classics

1. To be without some of the things you want is an indispensable part of happiness.
你追求不到的东西有时也是幸福不可缺少的一部分。

2. A man dies often as he loses a friend. But we gain new life by new contacts, new friends.
一个人每逢失去一个朋友就等于经历一次死亡。但是取得新联系，结识新朋友却又使我们获得了新的生命。

Change Your Bad Habit to Good—Modify Your Environment
改掉坏毛病，养成好习惯——改善周边环境

3. I do not like work—no man does—but I like what is in the work—the chance to find your self.
   我不喜欢工作，没有人会喜欢工作。但是我喜欢在所从事的工作中找到发现自己的机会。

4. I find life an exciting business and most exciting when it is lived for others.
   我发现生活是令人激动的事情，尤其是为别人活着时。

5. No one is safe from slander. The best way is to pay no attention to it, but live in innocence and let the world talk.
   任何人都不能免于诽谤。最好的方法是不理会，过着清白的生活，让人们去说好了。

6. Coward die many times before their death.
   懦夫在死之前，就已经死过很多次了。

7. We have no more right to consume happiness without producing it than to consume wealth without producing it.
   不创造幸福的人无权享用幸福，正如不创造财富的人无权享用财富一样。

8. It is better to waste one's youth than to do nothing with it at all.
   年轻时做一点儿事要比什么事也不做好。

9. Courage is resistance to fear, mastery of fear – not absence of fear.
   勇敢并非没有恐惧，而是克服恐惧，战胜恐惧。

10. Nothing in all the world is more dangerous than sincere ignorance and conscientious stupidity.
    世界上再也没有比纯粹的无知和认真的愚蠢更危险的了。

11. You should, like a candle, burn out yourself to give light to others.
    要像蜡烛一样燃烧自己，照亮别人。

20 Change Your Bad Habit to Good—Monitor Your Behavior
改掉坏毛病，养成好习惯——监督自身行为

I've been reading research studies on self-monitoring for 20 years, and I've conducted some myself. To be honest, I still don't fully understand why this technique works, but it does, and **remarkably** well for most people.

Use **gizmos**. If you say "you know" too much, wear a golf counter on your **wrist**, and press the button whenever you catch yourself saying "you know". I'll bet you say it less **frequently** in just a few days. If a wrist counter is embarrassing, then make a small tear in a piece of paper in your pocket each time you say "you know". The result is the same: you become more aware of what you're doing, and that makes you perform better.

If techniques like this sound silly, keep in mind that the power of **self-monitoring** has been demonstrated by a variety of research conducted over the last four decades. In a study I published in 1978 with Claire Goss, for example, we taught a **disruptive** fifth-grade boy to rate his own class-room behavior twice a day. He simply checked off a score for himself, indicating how well-behaved he

20年来我一直在阅读有关自我监督的研究报告，而且自己也做过一些研究。老实说，我仍未完全弄懂，为何自我监督这种方法行之有效，但它确实有效，而且对多数人都效果显著。

试着用一些小把戏吧。如果你总是把"you know"挂在嘴边，就在手腕上戴个高尔夫计数器，每当意识到自己说一次"you know"时就按一下计数键。我敢打赌，过不了几天，你就不会那么频繁地说起它了。倘若嫌戴腕部计数器令人难堪，那么就在每说一次"you know"时把口袋里的一张纸弄破一个小洞。其结果是一样的：你会变得更留意自己的行为，因而也就表现更佳。

如果说这样的方法听起来颇为荒唐，请记住：自我监督的力量已在40年来所进行的各种研究中得到了证实。我和克莱尔·戈斯于1978年发表的一篇研究报告中就有一个实例。我们教一个爱捣乱的五年级小男孩每天对自己的课堂表现做两次等级评定。他只是简单地

Change Your Bad Habit to Good—Monitor Your Behavior
改掉坏毛病，养成好习惯——监督自身行为

had been in the morning or afternoon. With his **awareness** increased, he stayed in his seat more than usual, completed more **assignments** and rarely got in trouble.

Working with emotionally disturbed children, Sonya Carr of Southeastern Louisiana University and Rebecca Punzo, a New Orleans teacher reported that self-monitoring improves **academic** performance in reading, mathematics and spelling. Recent research even demonstrated that students will compose better stories given a simple **checklist** that includes elements of good writing. Dozens of studies have similar results, all **spurred** by heightening our awareness of our behavior.

给自己打个分数，以表明自己上午或下午表现得如何好。随着自我监测意识的增强，他比平常更能待在座位上，完成的作业也更多了，而且很少再惹麻烦了。

东南路易斯安那大学的索尼亚·卡尔和新奥尔良教师丽贝卡·庞佐在研究过情绪失常儿童后发表报告称，自我监督能改善这些孩子在阅读、数学和拼写方面的学习表现。最近的研究甚至表明，学生只要得到一张含有优秀写作要素的简要清单，就能写出更好的故事来。大量研究都取得了类似的结果，而且都是通过加强自我行为意识而得出的。

单词解析 Word Analysis

remarkably [rɪˈmɑːkəblɪ] *adv.* 引人注目地，明显地，非常
例 The book, so far as I can judge, is remarkably accurate.
就我看来，这本书内容相当准确。

gzimo [ˈgɪzməʊ] *n.* 小发明
例 Thanks to a new gizmo, you now just need to face the music and dance.
幸亏有一项新发明，现在手机没电的时候，你只要临危不惧，翩翩起舞就可以了。

wrist [rɪst] *n.* 腕，手腕；腕关节；（衣袖等的）腕部
例 The fate line begins close to the wrist.

命运线始于接近手腕的地方。

frequently ['friːkwəntli] *adv.* 频繁地，屡次地；往往；动辄

例 Dry hair can be damaged by washing it too frequently.
干性头发洗得太频繁容易受损。

self-monitoring ['selfm'ɒnɪtərɪŋ] *adj.* 自行监控的

例 Self-monitoring strategy is an effective way of improving student's English comprehension.
在英语阅读中运用自我监控策略是一条提高学生阅读能力的有效途经。

disruptive [dɪs'rʌptɪv] *adj.* 分裂性的；破坏的；扰乱的

例 Alcohol can produce violent, disruptive behavior.
酒精会引发暴力和破坏性行为。

awareness [ə'weənəs] *n.* 察觉，觉悟，意识

例 Smokers are well aware of the dangers to their own health.
吸烟的人都知道吸烟对自身健康的危害。

assignments [ə'saɪnmənt] *n.* （布置的）作业；（分配的）任务

例 The assessment for the course involves written assignments and practical tests.
这门功课的考核包括书面作业和实际操作考试。

academic [ˌækə'demɪk] *adj.* 教学的，学业的（尤指学识方面而非实践、技能上的）

例 I was terrible at school and left with few academic qualifications.
我的学习成绩一塌糊涂，离校时几乎没有学历。

checklist ['tʃeklɪst] *n.* 清单；检查单

例 Make a checklist of the tools and materials you will need.
把你需要的工具和材料开一张单子。

spur [spɜː(r)] *v.* 鼓励；激励

例 His friend's plight had spurred him into taking part.
朋友的困境促使他投身参与。

Change Your Bad Habit to Good—Monitor Your Behavior
改掉坏毛病，养成好习惯——监督自身行为

语法知识点 *Grammar points*

① **To be honest, I still don't fully understand why this technique works, but it does, and remarkably well for most people.**

to be honest 老实说，说实话，相当于to be frank, to tell the truth。

例 To be honest, I was surprised he knew where I was, we moved so often.
说实话，我感到惊讶的是他知道我在哪里，我们搬家搬得这么勤。

To be honest I am still expecting more from me as well. But believe me, I do everything I can do.
老实说，我自己也在期待着自己的爆发。但是请相信我，我会做出一切努力的！

② **I'll bet you say it less frequently in just a few days. If a wrist counter is embarrassing, then make a small tear in a piece of paper in your pocket each time you say "you know".**

I'll bet 我敢打赌；我相信；我来猜一下

例 So, exactly how this works is up to you and your creativity. I'll bet that there's more than one good way to do this.
那么，究竟是如何工作的是由你和你的创造力决定。我敢打赌，有不止一个好的办法做到这一点。

Now, if I were to ask you, what was on the walls? I'll bet you can tell me.
现在，如果我问你，墙上是什么？我打赌你可以告诉我。

③ **He simply checked off a score for himself, indicating how well-behaved he had been in the morning or afternoon.**

句中check off a score "打分"，indicating "表明"，现在分词做伴随状语，how引导的感叹句做indicate的宾语从句。
现在分词短语做伴随状语出现的条件是：
1) 由一个主语发出两个动作；
2) 或同一个主语处于两种状态；
3) 或同一个主语发出一个动作时又伴随有某一种状态；
伴随状语的逻辑主语一般情况下必须是全句的主语，伴随状语与谓语动词所表示的动作或状态是同时发生的。

我的梦想美文：有梦想谁都了不起

伴随状语首先是一种状语，用来修饰动词的，同时是表示与谓语动词同时进行，即伴随着谓语动词的动作同时进行。

例 He said it angrily pointing at the notice on the wall.
他生气地说着，手指着墙上的布告。

这里，point与said同时进行，因此，pointing在这里是现在分词做伴随状语，表示主动和正在进行。

例 Having failed many times, he didn't lose heart.
有很多次失败，他没有灰心。

经典名句 Famous Classics

1. Happiness takes no account of time.
   幸福年华似流水。

2. Eat to live, but do not live to eat.
   吃饭是为了活着，但活着不是为了吃饭。

3. Talking much about oneself may be a way of hiding oneself.
   过多地谈论自己可能是隐藏自己的方式。

4. Civility is not a sign of weakness, and sincerity is always subject to proof.
   礼貌不是软弱的表现，真诚有待验证。

5. An honest man is the noblest work of God.
   诚实的人是上帝创造的最佳作品。

6. Books are the ever-burning lamps of accumulated wisdom.
   书籍是积累智慧的明灯。

7. Liberty is the right to do whatever the laws permit.
   自由必须受法律约束。

8. Practical wisdom is only to be learned in the school of experience.
   实用知识只有通过亲身体验才能学到。

9. The shortest way to do many things is to do only one thing at a time.
   要想多做成一些事情的捷径是一次只做一件事情。

Change Your Bad Habit to Good—Monitor Your Behavior
改掉坏毛病，养成好习惯——监督自身行为

10. The great end of life is not knowledge but action.
    人生的伟大目标不在于知，而在于行。

11. Saying and doing are two different things.
    言与行实乃两码事也。

12. He who would search for pearls must dive below.
    欲采珍珠须潜深水。

读书笔记

21 Change Your Bad Habit to Good—Make Commitments
改掉坏毛病，养成好习惯——许下诺言

At the University of California, my students and I surveyed more than 2,000 years of self-change techniques—perhaps most of the major self-change methods that have ever been proposed by religious leaders, **philosophers**, psychologists and **psychiatrists**. Here is what we found: Of the hundreds of self-change techniques that have been suggested over the centuries, perhaps only a dozen are **distinctly** different. Many have now been subjected to scientific study, meaning that researchers have tried to see which ones work best.

When you make a **commitment** to another person, you establish what psychologists call a **contingency** of reinforcement; you've **automatically** arranged for a reward if you comply and a **punishment** if you don't. It puts some pressure on you, and that's often just what you need.

For instance, if you want to exercise more, arrange to do it with a friend. If you don't show up, your friend will get angry, and that may be just the ticket to keeping you **punctual**. Decades of research have demonstrated the power of

在加利福尼亚大学，我和我的学生调查了两千多年来人们用来改变自我的技巧——也许主要方法中的大部分都是由宗教领袖、哲学家、心理学家和精神病专家提出的。我们的发现是：在几个世纪以来人们提出的几百种改变自我的方法中，也许仅有十来种与其他方法截然不同。许多方法至今一直是科学研究的对象，这意味着研究人员一直试图探明其中最有效的方法。

当你向别人许诺时，你就形成了心理学家所说的"后效强化"这么一种情况。一旦实现承诺，你自然早已准备好得到嘉奖；如果食言，面临的就是惩罚。这将给你带来压力，而通常这也正是你所需要的。

比方说，如果你想加强锻炼，那么就安排和朋友一起锻炼吧。假如你到时没露面，你的朋友就会生气，这或许正是督促你守时的一种手段。几十年的研究已证实了这一措施的效力。例如在1994年，弗吉尼亚理工学院和州立大学的达

Change Your Bad Habit to Good—Make Commitments
改掉坏毛病，养成好习惯——许下诺言

this strategy. For example, in 1994 Dana Putnam and other researchers at the Virginia Polytechnic Institute and State University showed that patients who made written commitments were far more likely to take **prescribed** medicine than patients who hadn't. Mary Lou Kau and Joel Fischer of the University of Hawaii reported a case of a woman who got herself to jog regularly by setting up a simple arrangement with her husband: He paid her quarters and took her out on weekends whenever she met her jogging goals.

There's good news here for all of us. We can meet many of the demands and overcome many of the challenges of life with simple skills—**straightforward** practices that anyone can master and that don't require **willpower**—in other words, with skill, not will.

纳·帕特南等研究人员证明，做出书面承诺的病人远比未做书面保证的病人更能按医嘱服药。夏威夷大学玛莉·卢·考和乔尔·费希尔报告过一位妇女的案例，这位女士使自己坚持慢跑锻炼的方法就是和丈夫达成了一项简短的协议——无论何时，只要她实现了慢跑目标，丈夫都给她一些零钱，并在周末陪她出去玩。

对我们大家来说这都是好消息。要满足生命中这诸多要求并克服众多挑战，我们只需运用简单技巧——而这些技巧是任何人都能掌握并且无需意志力的实践操作——换句话说，只用技巧，而非意志。

单词解析 Word Analysis

philosopher [fəˈlɒsəfə(r)] *n.* 哲学家
例 The philosopher speculated about the future of the human race.
那位哲学家考虑过人类的前途。

psychiatrist [saɪˈkaɪətrɪst] *n.* 精神病专家，精神病医生
例 Alex will probably be seeing a psychiatrist for many months or even years.
亚历克斯今后好几个月甚至几年都可能要去看精神科医生。

distinctly [dɪ'stɪŋktlɪ] *adv.* 明显地；无疑地；确实地；逼真地

例 However, many customers found the smell of this product distinctly off-putting.
然而，很多顾客觉得该产品有一股异味，非常难闻。

commitment [kə'mɪtmənt] *n.* 信奉，忠诚；承诺，责任，义务

例 Work commitments forced her to uproot herself and her son from Reykjavik.
她的工作迫使她和儿子从雷克雅未克搬走。

contingency [kən'tɪndʒənsɪ] *n.* 意外事故，偶发事件；可能性，偶然性

例 I need to examine all possible contingencies.
我需要审视一切可能出现的情况。
We have contingency plans.
我们有应急方案。

automatically [ˌɔːtə'mætɪklɪ] *adv.* 自动地；无意识地；不自觉地；机械地

例 Don't assume your baby automatically needs feeding if she's fretful.
不要想当然地认为你的宝宝一闹就是要吃奶。
The machine automatically downloads the required information to his or her fax.
机器能自动将需要的信息下载到传真机上。

punishment ['pʌnɪʃmənt] *n.* 处罚；惩罚

例 I have no doubt that the man is guilty and that he deserves punishment.
我毫不怀疑此人是罪有应得。

punctual ['pʌŋktʃuəl] *adj.* 严守时刻的，准时的，正点的

例 He's always very punctual. I'll see if he's here yet.
他总是很准时。我去看看他是否已经来了。

prescribed [prɪ'skraɪbd] *adj.* 规定的，法定的

例 Whatever regimen has been prescribed should be rigorously followed.

Change Your Bad Habit to Good—Make Commitments
改掉坏毛病，养成好习惯——许下诺言 21

不管制订的是什么样的养生计划，都要严格遵守。

straightforward [ˌstreɪtˈfɔːwəd] *adj.* 直截了当的；坦率的；明确的

例 The question seemed straightforward enough.
这个问题看起来够简单的。

willpower [ˈwɪlpaʊə(r)] *n.* 意志力；毅力

例 His attempts to stop smoking by willpower alone failed.
他多次想单凭意志力戒烟都没有成功。

语法知识点 *Grammar points*

① **Many have now been subjected to scientific study, meaning that researchers have tried to see which ones work best.**

be subjected to 受，遭受

例 Caged birds should not be subjected to sudden variations of temperature.
不要使笼中鸟遭受突然的温度变化。

There's no reason for users to be subjected to dialogs like these.
没有理由让用户忍受这样的对话框。

② **If you don't show up, your friend will get angry, and that may be just the ticket to keeping you punctual. Decades of research have demonstrated the power of this strategy.**

show up 到场；（使）清晰，（使）变得明显；（使）显现出来；使难堪，使尴尬，使丢脸

例 We waited until five o'clock, but he did not show up.
我们一直等到了5点，但是他始终没有露面。

The orange tip shows up well against most backgrounds.
橙色的尖端在大多数背景下都很醒目。

He wanted to teach her a lesson for showing him up in front of Leonov.
她在列昂诺夫面前让他难堪，他要教训她一通。

③ For example, in 1994 Dana Putnam and other researchers at the Virginia Polytechnic Institute and State University showed that patients who made written commitments were far more likely to take prescribed medicine than patients who hadn't.

be likely to 很可能，more是用来帮助likely构成比较级的，far用来修饰比较级

例 They would not be likely to alight on the surface of the sea.
它们大概不会降落于海面上。
People who truly loved once are far more likely to love again.
真爱过的人很难再恋爱。

④ We can meet many of the demands and overcome many of the challenges of life with simple skills—straightforward practices that anyone can master and that don't require willpower—in other words, with skill, not will.

此句中两个that都引导的是定语从句，修饰先行词straightforward practices。
in other words 换句话说

例 The mobile library services have been reorganized—in other words, they visit fewer places.
流动图书馆服务重新作了安排——换句话说，他们去的地方减少了。

经典名句 Famous Classics

1. Experience more than sufficiently teaches that men govern nothing with more difficulty than their tongues.
经验给我们太多的教训，告诉我们人类最难管制的东西莫过于自己的舌头。

2. Experience is the simply name we give our mistakes.
经验是每个人为其错误寻找的代名词。

3. Experience keeps a dear school, yet fools will learn in no other.
经验始终是收费高的学校，然而，笨汉非进此学校不可。

4. Experience never misleads; what you are missed by is only your judgement, and this misleads you by anticipating results from

Change Your Bad Habit to Good—Make Commitments
改掉坏毛病，养成好习惯——许下诺言

experience of a kind that is not produced by your experiment.
经验永远不会对你做错误的引导；把你引导错的只是你自己的判断，而你的判断之所以对你发生误导的作用，乃是由于它根据那种并非借着实验而产生的经验来预料的结果。

5. Experience without learning is better than learning without experiences.
有经验而无学问胜于有学问而无经验。

6. I have but one lamp wait which my feet are guided; and that is the lamp of experience. I know of no way of judging of the future but by the past.
我只拿一盏灯来指引我的脚步，而那盏灯就是经验，对于未来，我只能以过去来判断。

7. Mistakes are an essential part of education.
从错误中吸取教训是教育极为重要的一部分。

8. One thorn of experience is worth a whole wilderness of warning.
一次痛苦的经验抵得上千百次的告诫。

9. The tragedy of the world is that those who are imaginative have but slight experience, and those who are experienced have feeble imaginations.
世界的悲剧就在于有想象力的人缺乏经验，而有经验的人又缺乏想象力。

10. To make good use of life one should have in youth the experience of advanced years, and in old age the vigor of youth.
青年而有老年之经验，老年而有青年之朝气，就能使人生发挥更大的作用。

11. To most men, experience is like the stern light of a ship which illuminates only the track it has passed.
对于大多数人，经验像是一艘船上的尾灯，只照亮船驶过的航道。

22 We Need Dreams
我们需要梦想

We all want to believe that we are **capable** of great **feats**, of reaching our **fullest** potential. We need dreams. They give us a vision of a better future. They **nourish** our spirit; they represent possibility even when we are dragged down by reality. They keep us going. Most successful people are dreamers as well as ordinary people who are not afraid to think big and dare to be great. Dreamers are not content with being merely **mediocre**, because no one ever dreams of going **halfway**.

When we were little kids, we didn't dream of a life of struggle and frustration. We dreamed of doing something big and **splashy**, something significant. We dreamed big.

We know now that we have to put in the effort to reach our dreams, but the tough part is that most of us don't know where to start working. We might have every intention of becoming Vice President in five years or running across the finish line in a marathon or completing the novel we started years ago. But often we have no idea how to translate these dreams into actions.

我们都希望我们能成就伟大的事业，充分发挥我们的潜能。我们需要梦想。梦想给我们一个更好未来的想象。梦想可以滋养我们的精神；当我们被现实拖垮的时候，梦想为我们带来希望。梦想让我们继续前进。大多数成功人士都是梦想家，同时也是普通人，只是他们敢于梦想，敢于成就伟大事业。梦想者不满足于做平庸的普通人，因为从来没有人想过要半途而废。

当我们还是孩子的时候，我们没有想过我们的人生会充满斗争与挫折。我们都梦想过做一番大事业，做有意义的事情。我们的梦想很大。

我们知道我们必须努力实现我们的梦想，但是最困难的是，我们当中的大多数人并不知道从哪里开始。我们可能会打算在五年后成为副总统，或者跑完马拉松全程，或者完成我们多年以前开始写的小说。但是我们常常不知道怎样将这些梦想付诸行动。

为了使我们的伟大炫目的

We Need Dreams
我们需要梦想

In order to make real steps toward fulfilling our **ultimate**, big, splashy dreams, we have to start with **concrete objectives**. These are our goals.

终极梦想成为现实,我们必须从具体的事情做起。这就是我们的目标。

单词解析 Word Analysis

capable ['keɪpəbl] *adj.* 有能力的;能干的;有……可能性

例 Only human beings are capable of speech.
只有人类才具有说话的能力。
The kitchen is capable of catering for several hundred people.
厨房能同时容纳数百人进餐。

feat [fiːt] *n.* 技艺;功绩,伟业

例 Apparently impossible feats are now accomplished by science.
许多看起来不可能的伟大业绩现在已经由科学实现了。
A racing car is an extraordinary feat of engineering.
赛车是工程学上一项相当了不起的成就。

full of 充满……的

例 He delivered a long prose full of platitudes.
他发表了一篇充满陈词滥调的文章。

nourish ['nɜːrɪʃ] *v.* 滋养;给营养;培育;怀有

例 They needed good food to nourish their bodies.
他们需要好食品滋养身体。

mediocre [ˌmiːdi'oʊkər] *adj.* 平庸的;平凡的

例 This leads to mediocre training, fitness and performance.
这将导致平庸的训练、体能和成绩。

halfway [ˌhæf'weɪ] *adv.* 半路地;在……中间;折中地

例 The car began to get ahead halfway through the race.
那辆车在比赛的半途开始领先。

splashy ['splæʃi] *adj.* 大而显眼的；引人注目的
例 The celebrity couple had a splashy wedding in London.
那一对名人在伦敦举行了引人注目的隆重婚礼。

ultimate ['ʌltɪmət] *adj.* 根本的；极限的；最后的；终极的
例 Nuclear weapons are the ultimate deterrent.
核武器是终极的威慑力量。

concrete ['kɑːŋkriːt] *adj.* 具体的；实质性的；混凝土的
例 I can't tell you anything concrete.
具体的我也说不上来。
The builders have perched a light concrete dome on eight slender columns.
建筑工人在8根细柱上架起轻巧的混凝土穹顶。

objective [əb'dʒektɪv] *n.* 目标；目的
例 Her principal objective was international fame as a scientist.
她的主要目标是成为有国际声誉的科学家。

语法知识点 Grammar points

① **We all want to believe that we are capable of great feats, of reaching our fullest potential.**

这个句子中有一个that引导的宾语从句，从句做believe的宾语。
be capable of 有能力，能够
例 It wasn't until after we were married that I realized what depths of emotion she was capable of.
直到我们结婚以后，我才了解她是一个多么富有感情的人。

② **They nourish our spirit; they represent possibility even when we are dragged down by reality.**

drag down 拖垮
例 To fill in increasing order, drag down or to the right.
要按升序填充，请从上到下或从左到右拖动。

We Need Dreams
我们需要梦想 22

A construction bust will continue to drag down output growth.
新建屋减少会继续拉低产出增长。

③ Most successful people are dreamers as well as ordinary people who are not afraid to think big and dare to be great.

这个句子中有一个who引导的定语从句，先行词是people，who在从句中充当主语成分。

as well as 也，还，并且，和……一样（谓语与第一主语一致）

例 He shared in my sorrows as well as in my joys.
他分担我的快乐也分享我的悲伤。

be afraid to 害怕去做……

例 He dismissed his critics as pious do-gooders who were afraid to face the facts.
他把批评他的人斥之为不敢面对事实的假善人。

④ Dreamers are not content with being merely mediocre, because no one ever dreams of going halfway.

be content with 对……感到满意；满足于；以……为满足

例 It is better to be content with what one has than to risk losing everything by being too greedy.
最好满足于现有的，以免因贪心而失去一切。

dream of 梦想做……；梦见；渴望（后跟动名词）

例 Against all the odds she achieved her dream of becoming a ballerina.
她克服重重困难，实现了当芭蕾舞演员的梦想。

例 I'd never dream of allowing my child to do that.
我决不允许我的孩子做那种事。

经典名句 Famous Classics

1. Wearing your learning, like your watch, in a private pocket; and do not merely pull it out and strike it merely to show you have on. If you are asked what o'clock it is, tell it; but do not proclaim it hourly and unasked like the watch man.

应该像对待你的怀表一样对待你的学问：把它装在口袋里，而不是挂在外面炫耀。如果别人问你几点了，就告诉他；但是没人问你的话，不要像敲更人一样到了整点就报时。

2. We have no longer in any country a literature as great as the literature of the old world, and that is because the newspapers, all kinds of second-rate books, the preoccupation of men with all kinds of practical changes, have driven the living imagination out of this world.
在任何国家都不再有像古时候一样伟大的文学作品了，市面上充斥着报纸和各种二流书籍，人们都忙着去应对这个不断变化的现实社会，被榨干了生动的想象力。

3. The opposite of love is not hate, it's indifference.
The opposite of art is not ugliness, it's indifference.
The opposite of faith is not heresy, it's indifference.
The opposite of life is not death, it's indifference.
爱情的反面不是憎恨，而是无动于衷。
艺术的反面不是丑陋，而是无动于衷。
信念的反面不是谬论，而是无动于衷。
生命的反面不是死亡，而是无动于衷。

4. No man, for any considerable period, can wear one face to himself, and another to the multitude, without finally getting bewildered as to which may be the true.
没有人能在任何一个时期里，面对自己时戴一副面具，在别人面前又表现出另外一副嘴脸，而最终不为哪个才是真实的自我而迷茫的。

5. For people of average ability, modesty is merely candor; but for men of great talent, it is hypocrisy.
对于一般人来说，谦虚只是诚实的表现；而天才的谦虚，就是一种虚伪。

6. What the superior man seeks is in himself, what the small man seeks is in others.
君子求诸己，小人求诸人。

7. If the devil doesn't exist, but man has created him, he has created him in his own image and likeness.
如果魔鬼并不存在，而是人们臆造出来的，那么就是人们按照自己的模样而造的。

8. Seven Deadly Sins; Wealth without work, Pleasure without conscience, Science without humanity, Knowledge without character, Politics without principle, Commerce without morality, Worship without sacrifice.
人类的七宗罪：不劳而获的财富，没有羞耻的享乐，没有人性的科学，没有个性的学识，没有原则的政治，没有道德的贸易，没有祭品的膜拜。

9. Forgiveness is the fragrance that the violet sheds on the heel that has crushed it.
原谅就是被人踩了一脚的丁香花，在人的鞋底留下芳香。

读书笔记

23 What I Have Lived For
我为何而生

Three passions, simple but **overwhelmingly** strong, have governed my life: the longing for love, the search for knowledge, and **unbearable** pity for the suffering of mankind. These passions, like great winds, have blown me hither and thither, in a **wayward** course, over a deep ocean of **anguish**, reaching to the very verge of despair.

I have sought love, first, because it brings **ecstasy**—ecstasy so great that I would often have sacrificed all the rest of my life for a few hours for this joy. I have sought it, next, because it relieves loneliness—that terrible loneliness in which one **shivering** consciousness looks over the rim of the world into the cold **unfathomable** lifeless **abyss**. I have sought it, finally, because in the union of love I have seen, in a mystic **miniature**, the prefiguring vision of the heaven that saints and poets have imagined. This is what I sought, and though it might seem too good for human life, this is what—at last—I have found.

With equal passion I have sought knowledge. I have wished to understand

我的一生被三种简单却又无比强烈的激情所控制：对爱的渴望，对知识的探索和对人类苦难难以抑制的怜悯。这些激情像狂风，把我恣情吹向四方，掠过苦痛的大海，迫使我濒临绝望的边缘。

我寻求爱，首先因为它使我心为之着迷，这种难以名状的美妙使我愿意用所有的余生去换取哪怕几个小时这样的幸福。我寻求爱，还因为它能缓解我心理上的孤独，我感觉到心灵的战栗，如站在世界的边缘而面前是冰冷、无底的死亡深渊。我寻求爱，因为在我所目睹的结合中，我仿佛看到了圣贤与诗人们所向往的天堂之景。这就是我所寻找的，虽然对人的一生而言似乎有些遥不可及，但至少是我用尽一生所领悟到的。

我用同样的激情去寻求知识。我希望能理解人类的心灵，希望能够知道群星闪烁的缘由。我试图领悟毕达哥拉斯所景仰的"数即万物"的思想。我已经悟出了其中的一点

What I Have Lived For
我为何而生

the hearts of men. I have wished to know why the stars shine. And I have tried to **apprehend** the Pythagorean power by which number holds sway above the flux. A little of this, but not much, I have achieved.

Love and knowledge, so far as they were possible, led upward toward the heavens. But always it brought me back to earth. Echoes of cries of pain **reverberate** in my heart. Children in **famine**, victims tortured by oppressors, helpless old people a hated burden to their sons, and the whole world of loneliness, poverty, and pain make a mockery of what human life should be. I long to **alleviate** the evil, but I cannot, and I too suffer.

This has been my life. I have found it worth living, and would gladly live it again if the chance were offered me.

点道理，尽管并不是很多。

爱和知识，用它们的力量把人引向天堂。但是同情却总把人又拽回到尘世中来。痛苦的呼喊声回荡在我的内心。饥饿的孩子，受压迫的难民，贫穷和痛苦的世界，都是对人类所憧憬的美好生活的无情嘲弄。我渴望能够减少邪恶，但是我无能为力，我也难逃其折磨。

这就是我的一生。我已经找到它的价值。而且如果有机会，我很愿意能再活它一次。

单词解析 Word Analysis

overwhelming [ˌovəˈhwelmiŋ] *adv.* 压倒性地，不可抵抗地

> She felt an overwhelming desire to have another child.
> 她一心想再要一个孩子。

unbearable [ʌnˈbɛərəbl] *adj.* 无法忍受的

> War has made life almost unbearable for the civilians remaining in the capital.
> 对留在首都的平民来说，战争已使生活变得几乎不堪忍受。

wayward ['weiwəd] *adj.* 任性的，不定的，刚愎的

例 Good sense and duty counseled her to control her wayward spirit.
优秀的情感和责任劝告她控制住自己任性的情绪。

anguish ['æŋgwɪʃ] *n.* 苦闷，痛苦

例 A cry of anguish burst from her lips.
她突然痛苦地大叫了一声。

ecstasy ['ekstəsi] *n.* 狂喜

例 My father was in ecstasy when I won my scholarship.
我获得奖学金时父亲欣喜若狂。

shivering ['ʃɪvərɪŋ] *adj.* 颤抖的 *v.* 颤抖

例 I was sitting on the floor shivering with fear.
我坐在地板上，吓得发抖。

unfathomable [ʌn'fæðəməbl] *adj.* 深不可测的

例 For some unfathomable reason, there are no stairs where there should be.
不知什么原因，本该有楼梯的地方却没有。

abyss [ə'bɪs] *n.* 深渊，无底洞

例 How big is the abyss between what you think you are and what you actually are?
你对自己的认识和真实的你之间差别到底有多大？

miniature ['mɪnətʃə(r)] *n.* 缩图，小画像 *adj.* 小规模的，纤小的

例 He looked like a miniature version of his handsome and elegant big brother.
他看上去就像是他那个英俊儒雅的哥哥的迷你版。

apprehend [ˌæprɪ'hend] *v.* 理解；忧虑；逮捕；拘押

例 Police have not apprehended her killer.
警察还未抓获谋杀她的凶手。

What I Have Lived For 我为何而生

reverberate [ri'və:bəreit] v. 回响，反响，反射
- A woman's shrill laughter reverberated in the courtyard.
  一个女人的尖笑声在院子里回荡。

famine ['fæmin] n. 饥荒
- Thousands of refugees are trapped by war, drought and famine.
  成千上万的难民陷于战争、旱灾和饥荒之中。

alleviate [ə'li:vieit] v. 减轻，使……缓和
- Nowadays, a great deal can be done to alleviate back pain.
  如今，减轻背部疼痛可以有许多方法。

语法知识点 Grammar points

① These passions, like great winds, have blown me hither and thither, in a wayward course, over a deep ocean of anguish, reaching to the very verge of despair.

hither and thither 到处，向各处，忽此忽彼
- He wandered hither and thither looking for a playmate.
  他逛来逛去找玩伴。

reaching to the very verge of despair现在分词短语做状语的用法，表示方式，伴随情况及结果。
- The child fell, striking head against the door and cutting it.
  小孩摔了一跤，头在门上碰破了。
  He went out slamming the door.
  他走出去砰的一声把门关上。

② This is what I sought, and though it might seem too good for human life, this is what—at last—I have found.

This is what I sought, what I sought是从句做表语，在英语里叫作表语从句，表语从句指一个句子作为表语，说明主语是什么或者怎么样，由名词、形容词或相当于名词或形容词的词或短语充当，和连系动词一起构成谓语。最后一句话this is what at last I have found是一样的用法。

例 That's why he got angry with me.
那正是他对我生气的原因。
The problem is who we can get to replace her.
问题是我们能找到谁去替换她呢。

③ **Love and knowledge, so far as they were possible, led upward toward the heavens. But always it brought me back to earth.**

so far as等于as far as，可用作连词，表示情况达到某种程度，意为："远到……；就……而言；在……范围内"。

例 As far as I know he'll be away for three months.
据我所知（就我知道的范围而言），他将外出三个月。

④ **I have found it worth living, and would gladly live it again if the chance were offered me.**

worth doing sth. 值得做某事，常用的是be worth doing something

例 It's not worth getting angry with him.
和他生气不值得。

be worth sth. 用于表示"数量、持续时间等"的名词之后，表示某物价值多少金额。

例 The new car cost a lot of money, but it's certainly worth it.
买这辆新汽车花了很多钱，但确实物有所值。
The thieves stole one million pounds worth of jewellery.
窃贼偷走了价值100万英镑的珠宝。

经典名句 Famous Classics

1. Jane Austen was an extraordinary woman; to actually be able to survive as a novelist in those days—unmarried—was just unheard of.
简·奥斯汀是一个不寻常的女人；她能够以小说家的身份存在并且终生未嫁，这在当时是前所未闻的。

2. There is in every true woman's heart a spark of heavenly fire, which lies dormant in the broad daylight of prosperity; but which kindles up, and beams and blazes in the dark hour of adversity.

在每个真正的女人心里都有一星神圣的火苗,在富足的平日隐忍沉寂,而在艰苦的时刻到来时,就会熊熊燃烧起来,照亮黑暗。

3. A kiss can be a comma, a question mark or an exclamation point. That's basic spelling that every woman ought to know.
一个亲吻也许是一个逗号,一个问号,或者一个惊叹号。每个女人都应该明白这些基本拼写。

4. Who would give a law to lovers? Love is unto itself a higher law.
谁会给爱侣们立法呢?爱情本身就是更高的法则。

5. I remember my youth and the feeling that will never come back any more—the feeling that I could last for ever, outlast the sea, the earth, and all men; the deceitful feeling that lures us on to joys, to perils, to love, to vain effort—to death; the triumphant conviction of strength, the heat of life in the handful of dust, the glow in the heart that with every year grows dim, grows cold, grows small, and expires—and expires, too soon, too soon—before life itself.
我还记得自己年轻的时候和那种一去不复还的感觉——那种仿佛要比大海,比这个世界,比所有的人都要活得长久的感觉;那种诱惑我们走向欢乐,走向毁灭,走向爱情,走向徒劳——以致走向死亡的幻觉;对自己的力量所抱有的信心,在一捧尘土中也能感到的生命的炽热,年轻的心脏里跳动的火焰,他们随着年月,逐渐暗淡,逐渐冰冷,逐渐萎缩,然后熄灭了——在生命本身完结前就太早,太早地熄灭了。

6. Live as long as you may, the first twenty years are the most longest half of your life.
不管你活得多么久,二十岁以前的时光总是你生命的一大半。

7. Only a moment; a moment of strength, of romance, of glamour—of youth! A flick of sunshine upon a strange shore, the time to remember, the time for a sigh, and—good-bye! —Night—Goodbye!
只有那么一瞬间,一瞬间的力量,一瞬间的浪漫气息,一瞬间的荣耀,那一瞬间就完结了的青春!黎明的阳光已经照射在陌生的海岸上,要在这时把它们刻在记忆中,要在这时深深地叹息,也要在这时候——告别了!——黑夜——再见!

24 We're Just Beginning
一切刚开始

"We are reading the first **verse** of the first chapter of a book whose pages are **infinite**."

I do not know who wrote those words, but I have always liked them as a **reminder** that the future can be anything we want to make it. We can take the **mysterious**, hazy future and carve out of it anything that we can imagine, just as a **sculptor** carves a **statue** from a **shapeless** stone.

We are all in the position of the farmer. If we plant a good seed, we **reap** a good **harvest**. If our seed is poor and full of weeds, we reap a useless crop. If we plant nothing at all, we harvest nothing at all.

I want the future to be better than the past. I don't want it **contaminated** by the mistakes and errors with which history is filled. We should all be concerned about the future because that is where we will spend the remainder of our lives.

The past is gone and **static**. Nothing we can do will change it. The future is before us and **dynamic**. Everything we do will affect it. Each day brings with it

"我们正在读一本书的第一章第一行，这本书的页数是无限的。"

我不知道是谁写的，可我很喜欢这句话，它提醒我们未来是由自己创造的。我们可以把神秘、不可知的未来塑造成我们想象中的任何模样，犹如雕刻家将未成形的石头刻成雕像。

我们每个人都像是农夫。洒下良种将有丰收，播下劣种或生满野草便将毁去收成。没有耕耘则会一无所获。

我希望未来比过去更加美好，希望未来不会沾染历史的错误与过失。我们都应举目向前，因我们的余生要用未来书写。

往昔已逝，静如止水，我们无法再做改变。而前方的未来正生机勃勃，我们所做的每一件事都将会影响着它。只要我们认识到这些，无论是在家中还是在工作上，每天我们的面前都会展现出新的天地。在人类致力开拓的每一片领域上，我们正站在进步的起跑点。

We're Just Beginning 24
一切刚开始

new **frontiers**, in our homes and in our business, if we only recognize them. We are just at the beginning of the progress in every field of human endeavor.

单词解析 Word Analysis

verse [vɜːs] *n.* 诗，韵文；诗节，诗行；诗篇；圣经中的节
例 I have been moved to write a few lines of verse.
我因感动而写下了几句诗。

infinite [ˈɪnfɪnət] *adj.* 极多的；极度的
例 The most amazing thing about nature is its infinite variety.
大自然最让人惊叹的是它的无限多样性。

reminder [rɪˈmaɪndə(r)] *n.* 提示；使人回忆起某事的事物
例 Violence has broken out in the capital, a stark reminder that the religious tensions are refusing to go away.
首都爆发了暴力事件，这给了人们一个严酷的提醒——宗教紧张局势还在持续。

mysterious [mɪˈstɪəriəs] *adj.* 神秘的；难以理解的
例 A mysterious illness confined him to bed for over a month.
他得了一种神秘的怪病，卧床有一个多月。

sculptor [ˈskʌlptə(r)] *n.* 雕刻家，雕塑家
例 I know a sculptor who swaps her pieces for drawings by a well-known artist.
我认识一个雕刻家，她用自己的作品去换一位著名画家的画作。

statue [ˈstætʃuː] *n.* 雕塑
例 There are factors, however, that have cast doubt on the statue's authenticity.
然而，有些因素让人对该雕塑的真伪产生了怀疑。

135

shapeless ['ʃeɪpləs] *adj.* 不成形的；无定形的；样子不好看的

例 Aunt Mary wore shapeless black dresses.
玛丽姨妈总是穿一些没款没形的黑色裙子。

harvest ['hɑːvɪst] *n.* 收割；收获季节；收成；结果

例 There were about 300 million tons of grain in the fields at the start of the harvest.
收获伊始地里大概有3亿吨粮食。

contaminate [kən'tæmɪneɪt] *v.* 污染

例 Have any fish been contaminated in the Arctic Ocean?
北冰洋的鱼受到过污染吗？

static ['stætɪk] *adj.* 静止的；不变化的

例 Both your pictures are of static subjects.
你的两张照片拍的都是静止物体。

dynamic [daɪ'næmɪk] *adj.* 动态的，发展变化的；（人）精力充沛的，有干劲的

例 He seemed a dynamic and energetic leader.
他似乎是一个富有干劲、精力充沛的领导。
Political debate is dynamic.
政治辩论是不断发展变化的。

frontier ['frʌntɪə(r)] *n.* 边界；边境

例 It wasn't difficult then to cross the frontier.
那时穿越边境并不困难。

语法知识点 *Grammar points*

① We are all in the position of the farmer. If we plant a good seed, we reap a good harvest. If our seed is poor and full of weeds, we reap a useless crop. If we plant nothing at all, we harvest nothing at all.

in the position of 处在……位置上

We're Just Beginning
一切刚开始

例 You should feel them out in advance, and never be in the position of guessing what you think they want to see.
你应该事先就揣摩出投资者的想法,而不是凭自己的臆想瞎猜。

Standing in the position of being right is going to keep you feeling wronged forever.
站在正确的位置会让你感觉一辈子被人冤枉。

② I don't want it contaminated by the mistakes and errors with which history is filled. We should all be concerned about the future because that is where we will spend the remainder of our lives.

want it contaminated 动词的过去分词做宾语补足语,contaminated做it的补足语,it是want的宾语。with which history is filled 实际是be filled with结构,with提到先行词前了。

例 He found his hometown greatly changed.
他发现家乡变化很大。

He got his tooth pull out yesterday.
他昨天拔牙了。

The bottle is filled with water.
瓶子里装满了水。

③ We are just at the beginning of the progress in every field of human endeavor.

at the beginning of 处于……的开端;起初

例 If you do not, the report displays the row number at the beginning of every group.
如果不这样做,报告就会在每个组的开头处显示行数。

Recovery analyzes and scans the log at the beginning of recovery, since the last checkpoint.
在恢复开始时,从上一个检查点恢复分析和扫描日志。

in the beginning通常单独用作时间状语或定语,而较少跟of短语连用,其意义为"起初、在开始的时候",暗含着后来有变化的意思。

例 In the beginning we thought we'd never get it all arranged.
在开始的时候,我们以为不会把它全安排好。

我的梦想美文：有梦想谁都了不起

经典名句 Famous Classics

1. From the satisfaction of desire there may arise, accompanying joy and as it were sheltering behind it, something not unlike despair.
   当欲望被满足时，伴随着快乐，同时躲在它身后而来的，是一种很像是绝望的东西。

2. Most people get a fair amount of fun out of their lives, but on balance life is suffering, and only the very young or the very foolish imagine otherwise.
   大多数人一生中有许多快乐，但综合来说人生是痛苦的，只有年轻人和愚蠢之人才不这样想。

3. Time lost is time when we have not lived a full human life, time unenriched by experience, creative endeavour, enjoyment, and suffering.
   我们浪费的时间就是我们没有充实地生活的时间，没有亲身体验，没有去冒险，享受和感受痛苦的时间。

4. How many roads must a man walk down, before you can call him a man? The answer, my friend, is blowing in the wind. The answer is blowing in the wind.
   一个人要经历多少旅途才能成为真正的男人？这答案，我的朋友，正飘零在风中，这答案正飘零在风中。

5. One of the most obvious facts about grown-ups, to a child, is that they have forgotten what it is like to be a child.
   对孩子们来说，大人们最明显的特点就是他们已经忘了怎么去当一个孩子。

6. Three passions, simple but overwhelming, have governed my life: The longing for love, the search for knowledge, and unbearable pity for the suffering of mankind.
   我的人生被三种简单但又强有力的激情所统领：对爱情的渴望，对知识的探索，以及对人类所有苦难的切身之痛。

7. The dullard's envy of brilliant men is always assuaged by the suspicion that they will come to a bad end.

平庸之人对伟人们的忌妒，总会因为怀疑后者会以悲剧收场而稍有减轻。

8. Life's perhaps the only riddle that we shrink from giving up.
生命大概是我们唯一猜不透又不敢放弃的谜语。

9. A pile of rocks ceases to be a rock pile when somebody contemplates it with the idea of a cathedral in mind.
一堆石头，当有人把它们想象成一座教堂时，它们就不再只是一堆石头了。

10. To find a young fellow that is neither a wit in his own eye, nor a fool in the eye of the world, is a very hard task.
要找到一个既不觉得自己充满智慧，又不被这个世界认为很愚蠢的年轻人，几乎是不可能的事。

读书笔记

25 Sure You Can
相信自己

Remember when you were a little child trying to learn to walk? First you had to learn to stand: A process involving **constantly** falling down, and then getting back up. You laughed sometimes and cried at other times. Somehow there was a determination and **conviction** that you would succeed no matter what. After much practice you finally figured out how to balance yourself, a necessary requirement. You enjoyed this new feeling of power, you'd stand everywhere you could in your **crib**, by the **couch**. It was a **joyous** time you did it! You were in control of you. Now "the next step" walking. You'd seen others do it— "it didn't look that hard" —just move your legs while you were standing. Wrong—more **complexity** than you ever imagined. More **frustration** than anyone should have to deal with. But you tried, again and again and again until you figured this out. If people caught you walking, they applauded, they laughed, it was, "Oh my God, look at what he's/she's doing." This encouragement **fueled** you on; it raised your self-confidence.

还记得你小时候刚开始学着走路吗？首先得学会站立，这是一个不断摔倒又站起来的过程。有时候会笑，有时候也会哭。不知为何，总有一种一定会成功的决心和信念。在经过多次练习之后你终于明白怎样保持自身平衡，这也是一个必要的需求。在婴儿床上，在沙发旁，你很享受这种想站在哪就站在哪的感觉。那确实是一段充满欢乐的时光！你能控制自己。接下来的一步是走路。你看到别人走的时候没有那么难，只是站着然后动腿。大错特错，走路要远比你想象的复杂。所以你比任何人都沮丧。但是你一遍又一遍地尝试，直到你学会走路。如果你走路的时候有别人在场，他们会鼓掌，会笑，好像在说："太棒了，看他/她呀！"这种鼓舞激励你前进，并增强你的自信心。

Sure You Can
相信自己

But how many times did you attempt when no one was watching, when no one was cheering? You couldn't wait for someone to **encourage** you to take the next steps. You learned how to encourage yourself. If we could only remember this about ourselves today, remember that we can do anything we set our minds to if we are willing to go through the process, just like when we learned to walk. We don't need to wait for others to encourage us; we need to encourage ourselves. If you've forgotten how to do this, or feel like your self-esteem needs a **boost**, take a short journey back through your life— "look at your **accomplishments**, no matter if they were large or small," You met the challenge and figured out a way to succeed.

While going back, look for the little child you once were. Thank them for never giving up. As you wave goodbye, remember they will never give up on you. They have believed in you all of your life! Now you need to believe in you, too! Remember, today is the best day of your life because yesterday was and tomorrow may only be.

但又有多少次，在你尝试走路的时候，没有人在旁边看着你，鼓励你？你不能等着别人鼓励才走下一步。你学着自我鼓励。如果现在我们还能记得这些事情，记得为了克服困难我们可以支配自己的思想做一些工作，就像我们学走路一样。我们不需要等待别人的鼓励，我们需要自我鼓励。如果你不记得怎么去做，或是觉得你的自尊心需要加强，那就回顾一下你的人生，看看你那些或大或小的成就，那时你遇到挑战，总会找到通往成功的道路。

回顾的时候，找到曾经的那个小小的你。谢谢他不曾放弃。当你向他告别的时候，也要记得他永远不会放弃你。他一直相信你，相信你的人生！现在你也需要对自己有信心！记住，昨天曾经是，明天可能是，今天确实是你人生中最美好的一天。

单词解析 *Word Analysis*

constantly [ˈkɒnstəntli] *adv.* 不断地，时常地；时刻；常常；历来

例 We are constantly being reminded to cut down our fat intake.
不断有人提醒我们要减少脂肪的摄入量。

conviction [kənˈvɪkʃn] *n.* 坚信；定罪；信服

例 She holds deep religious convictions.
她有深刻的宗教信仰。

crib [krɪb] *n.* 婴儿小床；食槽

例 Walk softly as you approach the baby's crib.
当你走近婴儿小床时，步子轻一点。

couch [kaʊtʃ] *n.* 长椅；睡椅；长沙发；兽穴

例 Little Tom was lolling about on the couch eating sweets.
小汤姆懒洋洋地躺在睡椅上，吃着糖果。

joyous [ˈdʒɔɪəs] *adj.* 充满快乐的；使人高兴的

例 The poem is a joyous affirmation of the power of love.
这首诗以欢快的笔触肯定了爱情的力量。

complexity [kəmˈpleksəti] *n.* 复杂；复杂性；复杂的事物

例 I often reflect on the beauty and complexity of life.
我们经常思考人生的美丽与复杂。

frustration [frʌˈstreɪʃn] *n.* 挫折，失败，失意

例 Frustration, anger and desperation have led to a series of wildcat strikes.
挫败感、愤怒和绝望引起了一系列自发性的罢工。

fuel [ˈfjuːəl] *n.* 刺激

例 Higher salaries helped fuel inflation.
提高工资刺激通货膨胀。

encourage [ɪnˈkʌrɪdʒ] *v.* 鼓励，鼓舞；支持，促进，鼓动

例 When things aren't going well, he encourages me, telling me not

to give up.
事情进展不顺的时候，他鼓励我说不要放弃。

boost [buːst] *v.* 增加；推进；鼓励

例 This will be a great boost to the economy.
这对于经济发展将是一个巨大的促进。

accomplishment [əˈkʌmplɪʃmənt] *n.* 成就；成绩

例 By any standards, the accomplishments of the past year are extraordinary.
不管以哪种标准来衡量，过去一年都成果斐然。

语法知识点 Grammar points

① **Somehow there was a determination and conviction that you would succeed no matter what.**

这个句子中有一个 there be 结构，尽管后面是 "determination and conviction"，但是符合就近原则，所以谓语动词用单数。

例 There is a book, two pencils and some buttons on the table.
在桌子上，有一本书、两支铅笔和一些扣子。

同样符合就近原则的还有用连词either... or, neither... nor, whether... or, not only... but(also), or等连接的并列主语。

例 Either the boy or the girl knows him well.
这男孩或是那女孩了解他。

Neither money nor fame has influence on me.
钱和荣誉都不会让我动心。

Not only you but also he is wrong.
你和他都错了。

② **After much practice you finally figured out how to balance yourself, a necessary requirement.**

figured out 解决，了解，算出

例 And at least one parrot figured out something close to the mathematical concept of zero.

至少已经有一只鹦鹉能够理解一些与"0"相近的数学概念。
I have figured out how much during the week I spent.
我算出了这个星期花了多少钱。

> ③ **Remember that we can do anything we set our minds to if we are willing to go through the process, just like when we learned to walk.**

这个句子中有that引导的宾语从句，做remember的宾语；if引导的条件状语从句以及when引导的时间状语从句。

go through 经历；检查；浏览；通过，穿过；经历，遭受；履行，实行

例 I've gone through the elbows of my sweater.
我的毛衣的肘部都磨破了。
He thought it his duty to go through the papers.
他认为自己有责任检查这些文件。

经典名句 Famous Classics

1. Action is consolatory. It is the enemy of thought and the friend of flattering illusions.
   行动是可以慰藉的。它是思想的敌人，是幻想的朋友。

2. He who has a thousand friends has not a friend to spare, and he who has one enemy will meet him everywhere.
   有千百个朋友也不嫌多，只有一个敌人却到处可见。

3. Almost anything is easier to get into than to get out of.
   几乎所有事情都是进去容易退出难。

4. It matters not how a man dies, but how he lives.
   一个人怎样死去并不重要，重要的在于他怎样活着。

5. Without art the crudeness of reality would make the world unbearable.
   如果没有艺术，现实的粗陋将使世界无法忍受。

6. Other people's interruptions of your work are relatively insignificant compared with the countless times you interrupt

yourself.
别人对你工作的干扰与你自己无数次地打断自己相比，微不足道。

7. To sensible men, every day is a day of reckoning.
对聪明人来说，每一天的时间都是要精打细算的。

8. Don't believe that winning is really everything. It's more important to stand for something. If you don't stand for something, what do you win?
不要认为取胜就是一切，更重要的是要有信念。倘若你没有信念，那胜利又有什么意义呢？

9. Learning is an ornament in prosperity, a refuge in adversity, and a provision in old age.
学问在成功时是装饰品，在失意时是庇护所，在年老时是供应品。

10. The reading of all good books is like a conversation with the finest men of past centuries.
读好书，如同与先哲们交谈。

读书笔记

26 Catch the Star that Holds Your Destiny
抓住生命中的那颗星

Catch the star that holds your **destiny**, the one that forever **twinkles** within your heart. Take advantage of precious opportunities while they still **sparkle** before you. Always believe that your **ultimate** goal is **attainable** as long as you **commit** yourself to it.

Though barriers may sometimes stand in the way of your dreams, remember that your destiny is hiding behind them. Accept the fact that not everyone is going to approve of the choices you've made. Have faith in your **judgment.** Catch the star that twinkles in your heart and it will lead you to your destiny's path. Follow that pathway and uncover the sweet sunrises that **await** you.

Take pride in your **accomplishments**, as they are stepping stones to your dreams. Understand that you may make mistakes, but don't let them **discourage** you. Value your capabilities and **talents** for they are what make you truly **unique**. The greatest gifts in life are not purchased, but acquired through hard work and **determination**. Find the star that twinkles in your heart for you alone are capable of making your

当生命中的那颗星在你内心闪耀的时候，要学会把握它，永远相信只要自己持之以恒，就一定能够实现自己心中的梦想。

尽管通往梦想的道路上总有坎坷，你需要记住的是，你的命运就隐藏在那困难背后。学会接受这样的事实：不是每一个人都赞同你的选择。你要坚定自己的判断走下去。捕捉住那颗在你内心闪耀的星吧，它将引领你抵达自己的命运之路。沿那条路走下去，你就会发现那属于自己的美丽日出。

为自己的成绩自豪，因为它们是你通往梦想的阶梯。要知道你自己也会犯错误，但是可别因此而气馁。正确评价自己的能力，是它们令你与众不同。生活里最丰厚的礼物不是买来的，而是通过艰苦的努力和决心获得的。找到在你内心闪耀的那颗星吧。虽然你独自一人，但也有能力实现你最辉煌的梦想。对即得的怀抱希望并抓住那颗掌控你命运的星吧。

Catch the Star that Holds Your Destiny
抓住生命中的那颗星

brightest dreams come true. Give your hopes everything you've got and you will catch the star that holds your destiny.

单词解析 Word Analysis

destiny ['destəni] *n.* 命运，定数，天命
例 We are masters of our own destiny.
我们是自己命运的主宰者。

twinkle ['twɪŋkl] *v.* 使闪耀；闪耀
例 At night, lights twinkle in distant villages across the valleys.
夜间，山谷那头的遥远村落里灯光闪闪。

sparkle ['spɑːkl] *v.* 闪耀；发泡；活跃
例 The jewels on her fingers sparkled.
她手指上戴的首饰闪闪发光。

ultimate ['ʌltɪmət] *adj.* 最终的；根本的；极限的
例 He said it is still not possible to predict the ultimate outcome.
他说现在还无法预料最终的结局。

attainable [ə'teɪnəbl] *adj.* 可达到的；可得到的
例 It is unrealistic to believe perfection is an attainable goal.
相信完美可以企及是不现实的。

commit [kə'mɪt] *v.* 把……交托给；指派……作战；使……承担义务；犯罪，做错事
例 This is a man who has committed murder.
这是一个杀人犯。
They are sitting on the fence and refusing to commit themselves.
他们保持中立，拒绝表态。

judgment ['dʒʌdʒmənt] *n.* 判断；裁判；判决书；辨别力
例 I respect his judgement and I'll follow any advice he gives me.

我尊重他的判断能力，会接受他提出的任何建议。

await [əˈweɪt] *v.* 等候，等待；期待

例 He's awaiting trial, which is expected to begin early next year.
他在等候审判，预计明年初开始。

accomplishment [əˈkʌmplɪʃmənt] *n.* 成就；完成；技艺，技能

例 By any standards, the accomplishments of the past year are extraordinary.
不管以哪种标准来衡量，过去一年都成果斐然。

discourage [dɪsˈkʌrɪdʒ] *v.* 使泄气；使灰心

例 It may be difficult to do at first. Don't let this discourage you.
万事开头难，别因此而灰心。

talent [ˈtælənt] *n.* 天资；天赋

例 She is proud that both her children have a talent for music.
她为自己的两个孩子都有音乐天赋而自豪。
The player was given hardly any opportunities to show off his talents.
那位选手几乎没有得到什么机会展示自己的天赋。

unique [juˈniːk] *adj.* 唯一的；独一无二的

例 The area has its own unique language, Catalan.
这个地区有自己单独的语言，加泰罗尼亚语。

determination [dɪˌtɜːmɪˈneɪʃn] *n.* 决心；坚决；果断

例 Everyone concerned acted with great courage and determination.
所有相关人员都表现出了极大的勇气和决心。

语法知识点 *Grammar points*

① **Catch the star that holds your destiny, the one that forever twinkles within your heart.**

本句中包括一个定语从句和一个同位语从句。

Catch the Star that Holds Your Destiny
抓住生命中的那颗星

在复合句中用作同位语的从句叫同位语从句，常常跟在fact, idea, opinion, news, hope, belief等名词后面，用以说明该名词表示的具体内容，可以由名词、代词、短语及句子来充当同位语从句。

例 The news that our team has won the game was true.
我们队赢了那场比赛的消息是真的。
We are not investigating the question whether he is trustworthy.
我们不是在调查他是否可以信任的问题。
Have you any idea what time it starts?
你知道什么时候开始吗?

② **Though barriers may sometimes stand in the way of your dreams, remember that your destiny is hiding behind them.**

stand in the way of 妨碍，阻碍；阻住……的路
例 Don't let relatives stand in the way of your personal plans.
不要让亲人干扰了你的个人计划。
No mountains and seas can stand in the way of the friendship between our two peoples.
千山万水也不能隔断我们两国人民之间的友谊。

③ **For you alone are capable of making your brightest dreams come true.**

be capable of 能够
例 Computer simulations suggest the distress signal should still be capable of being detected.
在计算机仿真环境中，这种遇险信号仍旧能够被探测到。
He may be capable of jealousy when you have made superior progress in your work.
当你在工作中取得较大进步时，他也会嫉妒你。

come true 实现，成真
例 His wish to study music has come true at last.
他学习音乐的愿望这回算实现了。

经典名句 Famous Classics

1. Real love stories never have endings.
   真正的爱情故事从来不会结束。

2. The best proof of love is trust.
   爱的最好证实就是信任。

3. In our society, the women who break down barriers are those who ignore limits.
   在我们这个社会，女人们只有无视束缚，才能冲破束缚。

4. On rare occasions one does hear of a miraculous case of a married couple falling in love after marriage, but on close examination it will be found that it is a mere adjustment to the inevitable.
   我们偶尔会听说有些夫妇在结婚后才爱上对方，这像是一个奇迹，然而在观察之后，我们知道这只是迫不得已而做出的改变。

5. A homely face and no figure have aided many women heavenward.
   平凡的脸与平庸的身材，让许多女人都成就非凡。

6. They say marriages are made in Heaven. But so is thunder and lightning.
   他们说婚姻是上天的产物，但是雷电也是。

7. Almost no one is foolish enough to imagine that he automatically deserves great success in any field of activity; yet almost everyone believes that he automatically deserves success in marriage.
   没有哪个傻瓜会期望自己在任何领域毫不费力就一举成功，但几乎每个人都想要不费力地得到一段成功的婚姻。

8. If you are flattering a woman, it pays to be a little subtle. You don't have to bother with man, they believe any compliment automatically.
   如果你要恭维女人，最好别太夸张。但是对男人不用担心，他们什么赞美之词都相信。

9. Women do not find it difficult nowadays to behave like men, but they often find it extremely difficult to behave like gentlemen.
现在的女人们要像男人们一样做事并不难，但她们很难像绅士们一样做事。

10. People marry for a variety of reasons and with varying results. But to marry for love is to invite inevitable tragedy.
人们为了许多不同的原因结婚，也有不同的结果。但是为了爱情结婚，等于是开始了无可避免的悲剧。

读书笔记

27 The Farmer's Donkey
井中之驴

One day a farmer's donkey fell into an **abandoned** well. The animal cried **piteously** for hours as the farmer tried to **figure out** what to do. Finally, he decided the animal was too old and the well needed to be covered up anyway; so it just wasn't worth it to him to try to **retrieve** the donkey.

He invited all his neighbors to come over and help him. They each **grabbed** a **shovel** and began to shovel dirt into the well. Realizing what was happening, the donkey at first cried and **wailed** horribly. Then, to everyone's amazement, he quieted down. A few shovel loads later, the farmer peered down the well, and was astonished at what he saw. As every shovel of dirt hit his back, the donkey did something amazing. He would shake it off and take a step up.

As the farmer's neighbors continued to shovel dirt on top of the animal, he would shake it off and take a step up. Pretty soon, the donkey stepped up over the **edge** of the well and **trotted** off, to the shock and astonishment of everyone.

一天，农夫的一头驴掉进了一口废弃的井里。当农夫在想要怎么办的时候，驴凄惨地嚎叫了几个小时。最后，农夫决定，驴已经很老了，不管怎样也要埋葬的，所以不值得救它出来了。

他邀请了所有的邻居来帮他。他们每个人都拿了一把铁锹，开始把土铲到井里。驴意识到发生了什么，刚开始猛烈地痛苦地嚎叫。然后，随着几铁锹的土的落下，驴完全安静了下来。农夫向井内窥视，他震惊了，只见随着每一铲满满的土打在驴的背上，驴总能抖掉它们并且迈上新土层从而站得更高。

当农夫的邻居们继续铲泥土抛到驴子的背上，它抖落泥土，并踩在泥土上面。令每个人都感到震惊和诧异的是，驴一步步地向上，很快就超过了井的边缘，然后快速地跑走了。

单词解析 Word Analysis

abandoned [ə'bændənd] *adj.* 被抛弃的；无约束的

例 Like abandoned rage, the despair response seems counter productive.
正如被抛弃的暴躁，绝望的反应也让人匪夷所思。

piteously ['pɪtɪəsli] *adv.* 可怜地；凄惨地

例 She implored piteously, in a voice choked with sobs.
她用哽咽的嗓音苦苦哀求。

figure out ['fɪgjəraʊt] 想出；解决；理解；断定

例 It didn't take the children long to figure out the correct answer.
孩子们没有花很多时间就算出了正确的答案。
I can't figure out why he is absent.
我弄不明白他为什么缺席。

retrieve [rɪ'triːv] *v.* 恢复；挽回；取回

例 She tried to retrieve the situation by making profuse apologies.
她不住地道歉，力图挽回局面。

grab [græb] *v.* 抓住；攫取

例 Grab a seat and make yourself at home.
随便找个地方坐，别客气。
Let's grab a sandwich and go to see the film.
让我们赶快吃个三明治就去看电影吧。

shovel ['ʃʌvl] *n.* 铲；挖斗机；一铲的量 *n.* 铲；铲成；舀 *v.* 用铲子

例 He seized a shovel and went into the garden.
他抓起一把铁铲走进花园。
Shovel the snow away from the garden path.
把花园小径上的积雪铲掉。

wail [weɪl] *v.* 痛哭；发出似哭的尖声；悲叹

例 There's no use wailing about/over mistakes made in the past.
为过去的错误痛哭是没有用的。

peer [pɪr] *v.* 凝视；窥视

例 She peers through the mist, trying to find the right path.
她透过雾眯着眼看，想找出正确的路。

edge [edʒ] *n.* 边缘；优势；边；刀口

例 Look out! You could fall off the edge here!
小心！你会从边上掉下的。

trot [trɑːt] *v.* 小跑；快步走

例 The Donkey began to trot faster, then to gallop.
驴子开始小跑起来，后来变成疾跑。

语法知识点 *Grammar points*

① **Realizing what was happening, the donkey at first cried and wailed horribly.**

这个句子中，realizing what was happening是现在分词做伴随状语，the donkey和realizing是主谓关系。

例 Noticing what has happened, he still keeps calm.
意识到发现了什么，他仍然保持镇静。

② **The farmer peered down into the well, and was astounded by what he saw.**

这个句子中有一个what引导的宾语从句，what在从句中充当宾语。

peer down 向下看

例 Terrified of heights, George could not bring himself to peer down into the gorge to see the rapids below.
乔治站在高处感到害怕，不敢俯视峡谷下面的急流。

be astounded by 因为……而大吃一惊

例 Everyone was astounded by the results of the election.
人人都被选举的结果惊呆了。

She was astounded by the news that she had won the speech contest.
她听到自己赢了演讲比赛的消息，感到十分惊讶。

The Farmer's Donkey 井中之驴 27

③ With every shovel—full of dirt that hit his back, the donkey would shake it off and take a step up on the new layer of dirt.

这个句子中有一个that引导的定语从句，先行词是every shovel—full of dirt，that在从句中充当主语。

shake it off 摆脱；摇一摇；甩掉

> 例 This cold has hung on for weeks. I just can't shake it off.
> 我伤风已拖了好几个星期了，就是好不了。

take a step up 向上走一步

> 例 He has taken a step up in the hierarchy.
> 他的等级已升了一级。

④ Pretty soon, the donkey stepped up over the edge of the well and trotted off, to the shock and astonishment of everyone.

trot off 赶紧走，快速跑开

> 例 Now, you must be trotting off home.
> 现在你得赶快回家。
> The dog sniffed at the dead body and trotted off, following the scent track.
> 狗嗅了嗅尸体，然后追随臭迹跑去。

to one's shock/astonishment 令某人惊讶的是

> 例 To my shock/astonishment, it had completely disappeared.
> 使我惊讶的是，它消失得无影无踪了。

经典名句 *Famous Classics*

1. I measure the progress of a community by the degree of progress which women have achieved.
   我用一个社会中女人们所取得的成就，来衡量这个社会的发展程度。

2. In love, women are professionals, men are amateurs.
   在爱情中，女人是专业选手，而男人是业余选手。

3. There's no evidence whatsoever that men are more rational than women. Both sexes seem to be equally irrational.
   没有证据证明男人比女人更加理性，这两个性别都一样的不理性。

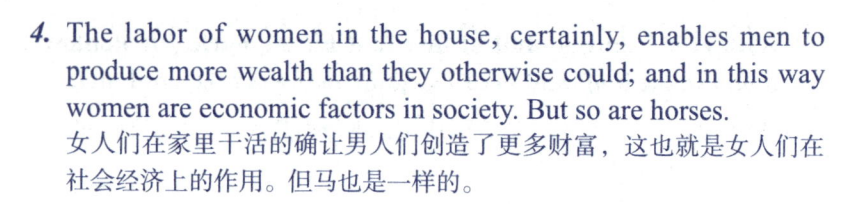

4. The labor of women in the house, certainly, enables men to produce more wealth than they otherwise could; and in this way women are economic factors in society. But so are horses.
女人们在家里干活的确让男人们创造了更多财富，这也就是女人们在社会经济上的作用。但马也是一样的。

5. They say that women talk too much. If you have worked in Congress you know that the filibuster was invented by men.
有人说女人们太唠叨。但如果你在国会工作过，你就知道，长篇大论是男人发明的。

6. Women with money and women in power are two uncomfortable ideas in our society.
富有的女人和有权势的女人，是我们的社会中两件让人不安的事情。

7. A man reserves his true and deepest love not for the species of woman in whose company he finds himself electrified and enkindled, but for that one in whose company he may feel tenderly drowsy.
一个男人并非为那种使他感到激情澎湃的女人们，才存有最深切的爱意；他们真正深爱的是让他们感到一丝困意的女人。

8. Years ago, manhood was an opportunity for achievement, and now it is a problem to be overcome.
许多年前，男子气概是成就事业的前提，现在却成了要克服的问题。

读书笔记

28 Feed Your Mind
充实你的思想

Since the pre-historic times, man has had an urge to satisfy his needs. Be it hunger, **shelter** or search for a **mate**, he has always **manipulated** the circumstances to the best of his advantages. Probably this might be the reason why we human beings are the most developed of all living species on the earth, and probably also in the **universe**. As we climbed the steps of evolution with giant **leaps**, we somehow left behind common sense and logical thinking—we forgot that we have stopped thinking ahead of time.

Hunger of the mind can be actually **satiated** through **extensive** reading. Now why reading and not watching TV? Because reading has been the most **educative** tool used by us right from the childhood. Just like that to develop other aspects of our life, we have to take help of reading. You have **innumerable** number of books in this world which will answer all your "How to" questions. Once you read a book, you just don't run your eyes through the lines, but even your mind **decodes** it and explains it to you. The interesting part of the

自史前时代起，人类就已有满足自己需求的强烈欲望。无论是饥饿、避难或寻觅配偶，人类总是操纵着环境使其达到最利于自己的状态。这或许解答了为什么人类是地球上甚至是宇宙中最高级的现存物种。然而在进化的阶梯上取得巨大飞跃之时，我们却不知何故将一些常识和逻辑思维抛诸脑后了——我们忘记了自己已经停止了超前思维。

事实上，思维的饥荒可以通过广泛的阅读来满足。为什么是阅读而不是选择看电视呢？因为自孩提时代起，读书就已经是最具教育性的工具了。正如人生发展的其他方面一样，我们不得不求助于阅读。世界上有无数书籍可以回答你"如何做"的问题。读书时不仅要用眼睛浏览文字，还要用脑去解读、诠释。书中有趣的部分就会像种子一样贮存在你的脑海里。将来你会不自觉地运用这粒种子引发新的想法。多次运用这粒种子将有助于你把许多事情联系起来，即使你做梦都想不到这些！

book is stored in your mind as a seed. Now this seed is unknowingly used by you in your future to develop new ideas. The same seed if used many times can help you link and relate a lot of things, of which you would have never thought of in your wildest dreams! This is nothing but creativity. More the number of books you read, your mind will open up like never before. Also this improves your **oratory** skills to a large extent and also makes a significant **contribution** to your vocabulary. Within no time you start speaking English or any language fluently with your friends or other people and you never seem to run out of the right words at the right time.

Actually, I had a problem in speaking English fluently, but as I read, I could improve significantly. I am still on the path of improvement to **quench** my thirst for satisfaction. So guys do join me and give food for your thoughts by reading, reading and more reading. Now what are you waiting for? Go, grab a book, and let me know!

这不是别的，就是创造力！你读的书越多，你的心智就会前所未有地开阔。而且这还会大幅度地提高你的演讲能力、丰富你的词汇量。你很快就能用流利的英语或别的语言与你的朋友或别人交谈，而且你再也不会在适合的场合缺少合适的词语。

实际上，我的英文还是不够流利，但只要我阅读，我就会取得显著进步。现在，我仍在自我提高，在头脑解渴的长路上跋涉。请加入到我的行列吧！通过阅读，阅读，再阅读，为你的思维喂食。你还在等什么？现在就拿起一本书让我瞧瞧！

单词解析 Word Analysis

shelter [ˈʃeltər] *n.* 避难所；庇护；庇护所

例 In the storm I took shelter under the tree.
暴风雨时，我正在树下躲避。

Feed Your Mind
充实你的思想

mate [meɪt] *n.* 配偶；伙伴；同事
例 I thought she was an ideal mate.
我认为她是我的理想配偶。

manipulate [mə'nɪpjuleɪt] *v.* 操纵；操作；控制；利用
例 He is one of those who manipulate the market.
他是操纵市场者之一。

universe ['juːnɪvɜːs] *n.* 宇宙；天地万物；经验领域
例 Einstein's equations showed the Universe to be expanding.
爱因斯坦的方程式表明宇宙正在膨胀。

leap [liːp] *n.* 跳跃；跃
例 The boy took a leap from the window.
那个男孩从窗口跳下去。

satiate ['seɪʃieɪt] *v.* 使饱足；使厌腻；充分满足
例 She pushed her chair back from the table, satiated.
吃饱了，她把椅子从餐桌处向后挪了挪。

extensive [ɪk'stensɪv] *adj.* 广泛的；广阔的；大量的
例 I have benefited a lot from extensive reading.
广泛的阅读使我受益匪浅。

educative ['edjukətɪv] *adj.* 教育的，教育性的，教育上的
例 Some of the advantages in their educational system have educative value.
他们的教育体制上的一些优势具有教育意义。

innumerable [ɪ'njuːmərəbl] *adj.* 无数的，数不清的
例 He has invented innumerable excuses, told endless lies.
他编造了数不清的借口和谎话。

decode [ˌdiː'koʊd] *v.* 解码；译解；译码
例 Method is used to decode the array of bytes.
方法用来解码字节数组。

oratory ['ɔːrətrːri] *n.* 讲演术；演说；祈祷室；小礼拜堂
- He dazzled the crowd with his oratory.
  他的演说使听众赞叹不已。

contribution [ˌkɒntrɪ'bjuːʃn] *n.* 贡献，捐赠，捐助
- He was awarded a prize for his contribution to world peace.
  他由于为世界和平做出贡献而获奖。

quench [kwentʃ] *v.* 熄灭；结束；冷淬；解渴
- Nothing could quench her longing to return home again.
  她重返家园的念头怎么也打消不掉。

语法知识点 *Grammar points*

① **Since the pre-historic times, man has had an urge to satisfy his needs.**

have an urge to do 有做某事的渴望或冲动
- He has an urge to become a cinema star.
  他渴望当一名电影明星。
  An urge to improve society led me into politics.
  推动社会进步的强烈愿望使我投身于政治。

satisfy one's need 满足某人的需求
- We must satisfy people's needs.
  我们要满足人民的需要。

② **As we climbed the steps of evolution with giant leaps, we somehow left behind common sense and logical thinking — we forgot that we have stopped thinking ahead of time.**

这个句子中有一个as引导的时间状语从句，表示"当……的时候"。后面还有一个that引导的宾语从句，作forgot的宾语。

leave behind 留下；遗留
- He left behind an immortal example to all posterity.
  他给后世留下了不朽的典范。

Feed Your Mind
充实你的思想

common sense 常识

例 He behaves as if he had no common sense.
他的言行就好像没有常识似的。

ahead of time 提前；提早

例 I have gotten my work all done ahead of time today, but I'd feel guilty going home while everybody else is still work.
我今天提早工作完，但是别人都还在工作，我不好意思回家。

③ **Just like that to develop other aspects of our life, we have to take help of reading. You have innumerable number of books in this world which will answer all your "How to" questions.**

just like 正如；几乎与……一样

例 Tom and I grew up here together, just like brothers.
汤姆和我一起在这里长大，情同手足。

后面句子中有一个which引导的定语从句，先行词是books，从句是对books的解释说明，which在从句中充当主语成分。

④ **More the number of books you read, your mind will open up like never before. Also this improves your oratory skills to a large extent and also makes a significant contribution to your vocabulary.**

open up 打开；开发；展现；开始；揭露；开放

例 Coughing like that might open up your wound.
你那样咳嗽会把伤口震开的。
The sales manager wants to open up new markets in the Far East.
销售经理想在远东开辟新市场。

to a large extent 在很大程度上

例 I agree with what you say to a large extent.
我很大程度上同意你所说的话。

make a significant contribution to 为……做出了重大贡献

例 This arrangement will make a significant contribution to increasing home ownership in Hong Kong.
这项计划可大大提高香港市民自置居所的比率。

经典名句 Famous Classics

1. The most beautiful things are those that madness prompts and reason writes.
最美丽的作品来源于疯狂,但用理智写成。

2. When I was the age of these children I could draw like Raphael; it took me many years to learn how to draw like these children.
我像这些孩子一样大的时候,我可以像拉斐尔一样作画;而我花了很多年才学会怎样像他们一样画画。

3. In a world full of audio visual marvels, may words matter to you and be full of magic.
在这个充满视觉与听觉享受的世界里,希望文字对你仍然充满意义与魔力。

4. Why does my Muse only speak when she is unhappy? She does not, I only listen when I am unhappy.
为什么我的缪斯只在悲伤中才对我说话呢?不是这样的,只是我在悲伤的时候才会听取她的话。

5. Only on paper has humanity yet achieved glory, beauty, truth, knowledge, virtue, and abiding love.
人类只有在书本中才创造了光荣、美丽、真理、知识、美德以及永恒的爱情。

6. In spite of everything I still believe that people are really good at heart. I simply can't build up my hopes on a foundation consisting of confusion, misery and death.
尽管发生了这一切,我仍然相信人们的本质是善良的。我无法将希望建立在混乱、痛苦与死亡之上。

7. You will know that forgiveness has begun when you recall those who hurt you and feel the power to wish them well.
当你回忆起那些伤害过你的人并且能够祝福他们的时候,你便知道自己已经学会了宽恕。

8. Beauty is eternity gazing at itself in a mirror. But you are the eternity and you are the mirror.
美来自于永恒对镜中的自己的凝视。但你是永恒,你是那面镜子。

29 Facing the Enemies Within
直面内在的敌人

We are not born with **courage,** but neither are we born with fear. Maybe some of our fears are brought on by your own experiences, by what someone has told you, by what you've read in the papers. Some fears are **valid,** like walking alone in a bad part of town at two o'clock in the morning. But once you learn to avoid that situation, you won't need to live in fear of it.

Fears, even the most basic ones, can totally destroy our **ambitions**. Fear can destroy fortunes. Fear can destroy relationships. Fear, if left unchecked, can destroy our lives. Fear is one of the many enemies **lurking** inside us.

Let me tell you about five of the other enemies we face from within. The first enemy that you've got to destroy before it destroys you is **indifference**. What a tragic disease this is! "Ho-hum, let it slide. I'll just drift along." Here's one problem with drifting: You can't drift your way to the top of the mountain.

The second enemy we face is **indecision**. Indecision is the thief of opportunity and enterprise. It will steal your chances for a better future. Take a

我们的勇气并不是与生俱来的，我们的恐惧也不是。也许有些恐惧来自你的亲身经历，别人告诉你的故事，或你在报纸上读到的东西。有些恐惧可以理解，例如在凌晨两点独自走在城里不安全的地段。但是一旦你学会避免那种情况，你就不必生活在恐惧之中。

恐惧，哪怕是最基本的恐惧，也可能彻底粉碎我们的抱负。恐惧可能摧毁财富，也可能摧毁一段感情。如果不加以控制，恐惧还可能摧毁我们的生活。恐惧是潜伏于我们内心的众多敌人之一。

让我来告诉你我们面临的其他五个内在敌人。第一个你要在它袭击你之前将其击败的敌人是冷漠。这是一种多么不幸的疾病！打着哈欠说："随它去吧，我就随波逐流吧。"这是多么可悲的疾病啊！随波逐流的问题是：你不可能漂流到山顶去。

我们面临的第二个敌人是优柔寡断。它是窃取机会和事业的贼，它还会偷去你实现更

sword to this enemy.

The third enemy inside is doubt. Sure, there's room for healthy **skepticism**. You can't believe everything. But you also can't let doubt take over. Many people doubt the past, doubt the future, doubt each other, doubt the government, doubt the possibilities and doubt the opportunities. Worse of all, they doubt themselves. I'm telling you, doubt will destroy your life and your chances of success. It will empty both your bank account and your heart. Doubt is an enemy. Go after it. Get rid of it.

The fourth enemy within is worry. We've all got to worry some. Just don't let it conquer you. Instead, let it alarm you. Worry can be useful. If you step off the curb in New York City and a taxi is coming, you've got to worry. But you can't let worry loose like a mad dog that drives you into a small corner. Here's what you've got to do with your worries: Drive them into a small corner. Whatever is out to get you, you've got to get it. Whatever is pushing on you, you've got to push back.

The fifth interior enemy is **overcaution**. It is the timid approach to life. **Timidity** is not a virtue; it's an illness. If you let it go, it'll conquer you. Timid people don't get promoted. They

美好未来的机会。向这个敌人出剑吧!

第三个内在的敌人是怀疑。当然,正常的怀疑还是有一席之地的,你不能相信一切。但是你也不能让怀疑掌管一切。许多人怀疑过去,怀疑未来,怀疑彼此,怀疑政府,怀疑可能性,并怀疑机会。最糟糕的是,他们怀疑自己。我告诉你,怀疑会毁掉你的生活和你成功的机会,它会耗尽你的存款,留给你干涸的心灵。怀疑是敌人,追赶它,消灭它。

第四个内在的敌人是担忧。我们都会有些担忧,不过千万不要让担忧征服你。相反,让它来警醒你。担忧也许能派上用场。当你在纽约走上人行道时有一辆出租车向你驶来,你就得担忧。但你不能让担忧像疯狗一样失控,将你逼至死角。你应该这样对付自己的担忧:把担忧驱至死角。不管是什么来打击你,你都要打击它。不管什么攻击你,你都要反击。

第五个内在的敌人是过分谨慎。那是胆小的生活方式。胆怯不是美德,而是一种疾病。如果你不理会它,它就会将你征服。胆怯的人不会得

Facing the Enemies Within
直面内在的敌人

don't advance and grow and become powerful in the marketplace. You've got to avoid overcaution.

Do battle with the enemy. Do battle with your fears. Build your courage to fight what's holding you back, what's keeping you from your goals and dreams. Be **courageous** in your life and in your pursuit of the things you want and the person you want to be.

到提拔，他们在市场中不会前进，不会成长，不会变得强大。你要避免过分谨慎。

一定要向这些敌人开战。一定要向恐惧开战。鼓起勇气抗击阻挡你的事物，与阻止你实现目标和梦想的事物做斗争。要勇敢地生活，勇敢地追求你想要的事物并勇敢地成为你想成为的人。

单词解析 Word Analysis

courage ['kʌrɪdʒ] n. 勇气；勇敢；胆量
例 They do not have the courage to apologise for their actions.
他们没有勇气为自己的行为道歉。

valid ['vælɪd] adj. 有根据的；正当的；合理的
例 They put forward many valid reasons for not exporting.
他们提出了很多不出口的正当理由。

ambition [æm'bɪʃn] n. 梦想；理想
例 His ambition is to sail round the world.
他的梦想是环球航行。

lurk [lɜːk] v. （通常指意图不轨地）潜伏，潜藏，埋伏
例 He thought he saw someone lurking above the chamber during the address.
他觉得自己看见有人在演讲时潜藏在会议厅顶上。

indifference [ɪn'dɪfrəns] n. 不感兴趣；不关心；冷淡
例 He laughed it off with aristocratic indifference.
他带着贵族式的漠然对其一笑置之。

indecision [ˌɪndɪˈsɪʒn] *n.* 优柔寡断；无决断力；迟疑不决

例 The team has been plagued by indecision and internal divisions.
优柔寡断与内部分裂深深困扰着该团队。

sword [sɔːd] *n.* 剑；刀

例 Fame can be a two-edged sword.
名声是把双刃剑。

skepticism [ˈskeptɪsɪzəm] *n.* 怀疑态度，怀疑论；多疑癖

例 The lips had already a little curl of bitterness and skepticism.
一缕辛酸和怀疑的神情，时时隐现在他的唇边。

overcaution [ˌəʊvəˈkɔːʃən] *n.* 过分小心，过分谨慎

例 You've got to avoid overcaution.
你要避免过分谨慎。

timidity [tɪˈmɪdətɪ] *n.* 胆怯，羞怯

例 He shows an almost childlike timidity in talking with strangers.
他和生人谈话简直像小孩子一样羞怯。

courageous [kəˈreɪdʒəs] *adj.* 勇敢的；有胆量的；无畏的

例 It was a courageous decision, and one that everybody admired.
那是一个勇敢的决定，也是一个为所有人赞赏的决定。

语法知识点 *Grammar points*

① We are not born with courage, but neither are we born with fear. Maybe some of our fears are brought on by your own experiences, by what someone has told you, by what you've read in the papers.

be born "出生"，动词be通常只用was或were，be born后可跟形容词、名词或不同的介词，表达意思也不同。

be born with 天赋；命运

例 He was born with a good memory.
他生来记性就好。

be born + of+（名词），表示"从……产生"。

例 This invention was born of need.
这项发明是因需要而产生的。

born + in / on等，表示"出生的时间、地点"。

例 Tom was born in London on February 12, 1999.
1999年2月12日汤姆生于伦敦。

be born + in, into或to，表示"降生到某家庭"。

例 In 1867 Madam Curie was born into a teacher's family.
1867年居里夫人出生在一个教师家庭。

② **But once you learn to avoid that situation, you won't need to live in fear of it.**

in fear of 害怕，担心

例 She lived in fear of her relationship with Dickens being exposed, but on Georgina she could always rely.
她一直害怕自己和狄更斯的关系被揭穿，但是她可以不需要担心乔治亚会泄露秘密。

③ **Worse of all, they doubt themselves.**

worse of all 更糟糕的是

例 Or worse of all, do you avoid her altogether?
或者更糟糕的，你会干脆回避她们吗？

经典名句 Famous Classics

1. We face the question whether a still higher standard of living is worth its cost in things natural, wild and free.
   我们面对的问题之一是：所谓"更高水平的生活"是否值得我们放弃自然的、充满野性和自由的生活。

2. Seize the day! Put no trust in the tomorrow.
   抓住眼前的光阴！不要相信明天。

3. But be not afraid of greatness: Some men are born great, some achieve greatness, and some have greatness thrust upon them.

不要害怕伟大：有些人生来就伟大，有些人通过努力达到伟大，有些人则不得不变得伟大。

4. I would rather be a superb meteor, every atom of me in magnificent glow, than a sleepy and permanent planet.
我宁愿做一颗华丽的陨石，完完全全地燃烧自己，发出光热，也不要做一颗永久沉睡的星球。

5. I don't think anyone, until their soul leaves their body, is past the point of no return.
我认为，一个人的灵魂只要还在身体里，不管它走得多远，都可以迷途知返。

6. Indecision is the thief of opportunity and enterprise.
优柔寡断是窃取机会和事业的贼。

7. Remember that the most beautiful things in the world are the most useless, peacocks and lilies for instance.
记住世上那些最美丽的东西都是最没用处的，比如孔雀和百合。

8. To desire and expect nothing for oneself and to have profound sympathy for others is genuine holiness.
真正的高贵是清心寡欲却又对他人怀有深切同情的人。

9. All my life I have tried to pluck a thistle and plant a flower wherever the flower would grow in thought and mind.
我的一生中，在每一个思想能够开花的角落，都试图拔出荆棘，种上鲜花。

10. It is wonderful how much time good people spend fighting the devil. If they would only expend the same amount of energy loving their fellow men, the devil would die in his own tracks of ennui.
人们能这样卖力地与邪恶奋斗真是太好了，但是如果他们能以这样的能量去爱他们的同胞，那么邪恶就自然会在苦闷中死去了。

30 On Idleness
论懒惰

There are some that **profess** idleness in its full dignity, who call themselves the idle, who **boast** that they do nothing, and thank their stars that they have nothing to do; who sleep every night till they can sleep no longer, and rise only that exercise may enable them to sleep again; who **prolong** the **reign** of darkness by double curtains, and never see the sun but to tell him how they hate his **beams;** whose whole labor is to vary the **postures** of **indulgence**, and whose day differs from their night but as a couch or chair differs from a bed.

These are the true and open votaries of idleness, for whom she weaves the **garlands** of poppies, and into whose cup she pours the waters of **oblivion;** who exist in a state of **unruffled** stupidity, forgetting and forgotten; who have long ceased to live, and at whole death the survivors can only say, that they have ceased to breathe.

But idleness **predominates** in many lives where it is not suspected; for being a vice which terminates in itself, it may be enjoyed without injury to others; and

有一些人声称懒惰也有它充分的尊严，这些人叫自己懒人，他们吹嘘自己什么都不做，也感谢上帝他们什么都不用做；他们每晚都睡到自然醒，然后做一些运动，只有那样他们才能再次入睡；他们用两层窗帘延长黑暗的时间，从来不见太阳却告诉太阳他们讨厌它的光；他们所做的一切就是变换一下沉昏的姿态，对于他们来说，白天黑夜的区别只不过相当于从沙发或椅子上挪到床上。

这些人是懒散女神真正公开的崇拜者，女神为他们佩戴罂粟花环，在他们的杯子里倾倒忘却之水；他们浑浑噩噩地活着，度日如年，忘却了他人也被他人所遗忘；他们早就停止了生活，他们死去时，活着的人也只会说他们不再呼吸。

懒散主宰了许多人的生活，而不为人所知；作为一种恶习，在不伤害他人的情况下被享受着；因而人们对懒散不像对危及他人财产的诈骗和自然而然地在从他人的自卑中寻

it is therefore not watched like fraud, which endangers property, or like pride, which naturally seeks it gratifications in another's **inferiority**. Idleness is a silent and peaceful quality that neither raises envy by **ostentation**, nor hatred by opposition; and therefore nobody is busy to censure or detest it.

There are others to whom idleness **dictates** another expedient, by which life may be passed unprofitably away without the **tediousness** of many vacant hours. The art is, to fill the day with petty business, to have always something in hand which may raise curiosity, but not **solicitude**, and keep the mind in a state of action, but not of labor.

No man is so much open to conviction as the idler, but there is none on whom it operates so little. What will be the effect of this paper I know: Perhaps he will read it and laugh, and light the fire in his furnace**;** but my hope is that he will quit his **trifles**, and betake himself to **rational** and useful diligence.

求满足的骄傲那样保持警惕。懒散不显山不露水，既不会由于炫耀而招致嫉妒，也不会因为对抗而遭人憎恨。正因为如此，没有人指责它，憎恶它。

对于其他一些人来说，懒散还有另一种表现形式，时光纵然白白流逝，而他们并没有因为许多小时没有做什么而感到无聊乏味。其办法就是一天到晚忙于琐事，手边总有事或许会激发起好奇心，却不会让他们牵肠挂肚；大脑总是动个不停，却不会让他们劳神伤思。

没有人愿意承认自己懒，但也几乎没人不受其影响。我不知道这篇文章将会产生什么影响：也许一个人读过之后，哈哈大笑，点燃炉火；但是我希望他能放下琐事，把自己投入到理性的、有用的勤奋工作当中。

单词解析 Word Analysis

profess [prəˈfes] v. 声称；冒称；表达，表明（感情、观点、信仰等）

例 They have become what they profess to scorn.
他们成了自己曾声称看不起的那种人。

boast [boʊst] *v.* 自夸；吹牛；以……为荣

例 Nobody should boast of his learning.
谁也不应当夸耀自己的学识。

prolong [prəˈlɔːŋ] *v.* 延长；拖延

例 How can we endeavor to prolong the brevity of human life?
我们怎样才能延长短促的人生？

reign [reɪn] *n.* 君主统治；在位期

例 People will remember the tyrannies of his reign.
人们不会忘记他统治时期的暴行。

beam [biːm] *n.* 光线；（光线的）束；（横）梁

例 Hold the flashlight so that the beam shines straight down on a sheet of white paper.
手握电筒让光线直射在一张白纸上。

posture [ˈpɑːstʃər] *n.* 姿势；态度；情形

例 Only humans have a natural upright posture.
只有人类才有自然直立的姿势。

indulgence [ɪnˈdʌldʒəns] *n.* 沉溺；放纵；嗜好

例 I must ask the readers' kind indulgence for any inaccuracies and omissions that may possibly occur.
我必须请求读者原谅可能出现的错误和疏漏。

garland [ˈɡɑːrlənd] *n.* 花环

例 I wove a garland of flowers.
我编了一个花环。

oblivion [əˈblɪviən] *n.* 遗忘；忘却

例 Many ancient cities are buried in oblivion.
许多古城都已被遗忘了。

unruffled [ʌnˈrʌfld] *adj.* 平静的；镇定的；沉着的；无波浪的

例 He remained unruffled by the charges.
他受到这些指控仍处之泰然。

predominate [prɪˈdɑːmɪneɪt] v. 占优势；支配
例 Pine trees predominate the woods here.
这儿的树林中最多的是松树。

inferiority [ɪnˌfɪriˈɔːrəti] n. 自卑；低劣
例 Failure induces a total sense of inferiority.
失败使人产生自卑。

ostentation [ˌɑːstenˈteɪʃn] n. 卖弄；虚饰；炫耀
例 The statue had beauty without ostentation.
那座雕像有一种不浮夸的美。

dictate [ˈdɪkteɪt] v. 口授；规定；决定，影响
例 You can't dictate to people how they should live.
不能强行规定人们应该怎样生活。

tediousness [ˈtiːdiəsnəs] n. 乏味
例 The clock dragged away the minutes teasing her with the tediousness of the day.
钟摇摆着一分分地过去，好像在嘲弄她乏味的一天。

solicitude [səˈlɪsɪtuːd] n. 关心；挂念；焦虑
例 His future is my greatest solicitude.
他的前途是我最关心的问题。

trifle [ˈtraɪfl] n. 琐事；少量
例 They had an altercation about a trifle.
他们为一点小事争吵起来。

rational [ˈræʃnəl] adj. 合理的；理性的；能推理的
例 Your choice was perfectly rational under the circumstances.
在那种情况下，你的选择是相当合理的。

On Idleness
论懒惰

语法知识点 *Grammar points*

① **But idleness predominates in many lives where it is not suspected; for being a vice which terminates in it, it may be enjoyed without injury to others; and it therefore not watched like fraud, which endangers property, or like pride, which naturally seeks it gratifications in another's inferiority.**

这个句子是一个复杂的复合句。首先是一个where引导的定语从句，先行词是many lives；后面是一个which引导的定语从句和两个which引导的非限制性定语从句。

without injury 无损伤

例 Wash the speck out without injury to your eyes.
把微粒洗出来，但不能损伤眼睛。

② **Idleness is a silent and peaceful quality that neither raises envy by ostentation, nor hatred by opposition; and therefore nobody is busy to censure or detest it.**

这个句子中有一个that引导的定语从句，先行词是a silent and peaceful quality，that在从句中充当主语。

neither... nor... 既不……也不……

例 It is neither hot nor cold in winter here.
这里的冬天既不热也不冷。

He has neither prepared his lesson nor gone to bed.
他没有准备功课也没有睡觉。

③ **No man is so much open to conviction as the idler, but there is none on whom it operates so little.**

not so much... as... 与其说是……不如说是……
so much as 甚至；几乎

例 I lay down not so much to sleep as to think.
我躺下来与其说是要睡觉，倒不如说是要思考。

It is not the boy that talks so much as the girl.
男孩几乎都没有女孩那么能说。

173

经典名句 Famous Classics

1. We have grasped the mystery of the atom and rejected the Sermon on the Mount.
   我们掌握了原子的奥妙,而放弃了山上圣训。

2. Egotism is the anesthetic that dulls the pain of stupidity.
   自大是一种麻醉药,让人察觉不到自己的愚蠢。

3. Selfish persons are incapable of loving others, but they are not capable of loving themselves either.
   自私的人无法去爱他人,但也无法爱自己。

4. He who is in love with himself has at least this advantage—he won't encounter many rivals.
   自恋的好处是不会有太多情敌。

5. Virtue is an angel, but she is a blind one, and must ask knowledge to show her the pathway that leads to her goal.
   美德是一位天使,但她是盲目的,必须要由知识带路才能到达目的地。

6. We can always make ourselves liked provided we are likable, but we cannot always make ourselves esteemed, no matter what our merits are.
   可爱的人总会被人喜欢;但无论是品德多么高尚的人,都不总是能受人尊敬。

7. Cruelty is perhaps the worst kind of sin. Intellectual cruelty is certainly the worst kind of cruelty.
   残忍也许是最坏的罪行。但对智力的摧残则一定是最恶劣的残忍。

8. Men have to do some awfully mean things to keep up their respectability.
   人们不得不做出一些非常恶劣的事情来维护自己的名望。

31 Where There Is a Will, There Is a Way
心中有目标，风雨不折腰

I used to watch her from my kitchen window, she seemed so small as she **muscled** her way through the crowd of boys on the playground. The school was across the street from our home and I would often watch the kids as they played during **recess**. A sea of children, and yet to me, she stood out from them all.

Well, I had to give it to her—she was determined. I watched her through those junior high years and into high school. Every week, she led her **varsity** team to victory.

One day in her senior year, I saw her sitting in the grass, head **cradled** in her arms. I walked across the street and sat down in the cool grass beside her. Quietly I asked what was wrong. "Oh, nothing," came to a soft reply. "I'm just too short." The coach told her that at "5.5" she would probably never get to play for a top ranked team—much less offered a **scholarship**—so she should stop dreaming about college.

She was **heartbroken** and I felt my own throat tighten as I sensed her **disappointment**. I asked her if she had talked to her dad about it yet. She lifted

我以前常常从我家厨房的窗户看到她，她强行挤过操场上的一群男孩，对这些男孩们来说，她显得那么矮小。学校在我家的街对面，我经常看到孩子们在下课时间打球。尽管有一大群的孩子，但我觉得她是最吸引我注意的一个。

嘿，我真服了她——她是个有决心的人。我看着她这些年从初中升到高中。每个星期，由她带领的学校篮球队都能够获胜。

在她读高中的某一天，我看见她坐在草地上，头埋在臂弯里。因此，我穿过街道，坐到她旁边的清凉的草地上，轻轻地问她发生了什么事。她轻声回答："哦，没什么，只是我太矮了。"原来篮球教练告诉她，以她五尺五英寸的身材，几乎是没有机会到一流的球队去打球的，更不用说会获得奖学金了，所以她应该放弃想上大学的梦想。

她很伤心，由于感受到了她的失望，我也觉得自己的喉咙发紧。我问她是否与她的爸爸谈过这件事。她从臂弯里抬

her head from her hands and told me that her father said those coaches were wrong. They just didn't understand the power of a dream. He told her that if she really wanted to play for a good college, if she truly wanted a scholarship, that nothing could stop her except one thing—her own **attitude**. He told her again, "if the dream is big enough, the facts don't count."

The next year, as she and her team went to the Northern California Championship game, she was seen by a college **recruiter.** She was indeed offered a scholarship, a full ride, to a Division I, NCAA women's basketball team. She was going to get the college education that she had dreamed of and worked toward for all those years.

It's true: If the dream is big enough, the facts don't count.

起头，告诉我，她父亲说那些教练讲得不对。他们根本不懂得梦想的力量。她父亲说，如果她真的有心去代表一个好的大学打篮球，如果她真的想获得奖学金，任何东西也不能阻止她，除非她自己没有这个心。他又一次跟她说："如果梦想远大，就一定可以克服艰难险阻。"

第二年，当她和她的球队去参加北加利福尼亚州冠军赛时，她被一位大学的招生人员看中了。那所大学真的为她提供了一份全面资助的奖学金，并且她进入了美国全国大学体育协会其中一个女子甲组篮球队。她将接受她梦想的并为之奋斗了多年的大学教育。

这句话说得真好：如果梦想远大，就一定可以克服艰难险阻。

单词解析 Word Analysis

muscle ['mʌsl] v. 强行向前

例 He muscled his way into the office.
他强行进入办公室。

recess [rɪ'ses] n. 课间休息；休会，休庭

例 The conference broke for a recess.
会议暂时休会。
The hearings have now recessed for dinner.
听证会现已休会就餐。

Where There Is a Will, There Is a Way
心中有目标，风雨不折腰

varsity ['vɑːsəti] *n.* 大学（尤指牛津或剑桥）；（学校的）代表队

例 The school has not given them the same opportunities to participate in varsity sports that men receive.
学校没有给她们与男生同样多的参加大学体育活动的机会。

senior ['siːniə(r)] *adj.* （级别、地位等）较高的；资深的；年长的；<美>最高年级的

例 The position had to be filled by an officer senior to Haig.
这个位置必须由一个职位高于黑格的官员来担任。

cradle ['kreɪdl] *v.* 将……置于摇篮中；轻轻地抱或捧；抚养；把……搁在支架上

例 He was sitting at the big table cradling a large bowl of milky coffee.
他坐在一张大桌子旁，手里捧着一大碗加了牛奶的咖啡。

scholarship ['skɒləʃɪp] *n.* 奖学金

例 He got a scholarship to the Pratt Institute of Art.
他获得了普拉特艺术学院的奖学金。

heartbroken ['hɑːtbrəʊkən] *adj.* 极度伤心的；心碎的；悲痛欲绝的

例 Was your daddy heartbroken when they got a divorce?
他们离婚时你爸爸是不是很伤心？

disappointment [ˌdɪsə'pɔɪntmənt] *n.* 失望；沮丧；扫兴

例 Despite winning the title, their last campaign ended in great disappointment.
尽管赢得了冠军，但他们最后一役却令人大失所望。

attitude ['ætɪtjuːd] *n.* 态度，看法

例 Being unemployed produces negative attitudes to work.
失业会产生对工作的消极态度。

recruiter [rɪ'kruːtə(r)] *v.* 大学的招生人员

例 The police are trying to recruit more black and Asian officers.
警方正在试图招募更多黑人和亚裔警官。

177

语法知识点 *Grammar points*

① **The coach told her that at "5.5" she would probably never get to play for a top ranked team—much less offered a scholarship—so she should stop dreaming about college.**

much less 更不用说

例 I never think of it, much less say it.
我想都未想到它,更不用说讲到它了。
She wouldn't take a drink, much less stay for dinner.
她连饮料都不愿喝一杯,更别提留下吃饭了。

类似用法还有even less, still less

例 He can't read English, still less can he teach it.
他看都看不懂英语,更不用说教了。
She can't finish her own work in time, even less help others.
她连自己的工作都不能及时完成,更不用说帮助别人了。

② **She was heartbroken and I felt my own throat tighten as I sensed her disappointment.**

feel sth. done, feel之后用过去分词的复合结构。

例 He felt a great weight taken off his mind.
他感觉去掉了一件心头大事。

feel后面也通常接现在分词的复合结构,即feel sb. /sth. doing

例 We all felt the house shaking.
我们都感觉房子在摇晃。

③ **He told her that if she really wanted to play for a good college, if she truly wanted a scholarship, that nothing could stop her except one thing—her own attitude.**

本句的宾语从句里面包含了两个 if 引导的条件句,且两个条件句是并列的,通过这两个并列的条件句引出了后面宾语从句里的主句。两个并列条件句形成了对比,加强了语气,从而使后面引出的句子显得更加突出。

④ **It's true: If the dream is big enough, the facts don't count.**

It's true... 或It's true that...,通过这样的句式可以表达对某事的总结或自己的感想或体会。

Where There Is a Will, There Is a Way
心中有目标，风雨不折腰 31

例 It is true that the whole world is witnessing China's construction of modernization.
中国的现代化建设确实正为全世界所关注。

经典名句 Famous Classics

1. War grows out of the desire of the individual to gain advantage at the expense of his fellow man.
战争来自于为了自己的利益而牺牲自己的同胞的意愿。

2. Indifference is a militant thing. It batters down the walls of cities and murders the women and children amid the flames and the purloining of altar vessels.
冷漠是一种好战的特征。它摧毁城墙，在熊熊大火中屠杀妇女与孩童，并且偷走圣坛上的罐子。

3. Morality knows nothing of geographical boundaries or distinctions of race.
道德没有地理领域和民族血统的界限。

4. Clever people will recognize and tolerate nothing but cleverness.
聪明人除了聪明本身之外，什么都无法接受和忍耐。

5. Hard work spotlights the character of people: Some turn up their sleeves, some turn up their noses, and some don't turn up at all.
艰苦的工作能显露人们的本性：一些人挽起袖子，一些人避开目光，一些人则根本不到场。

6. If you modestly enjoy your fame you are not unworthy to rank with the holy.
如果你能谦逊地对待名利，那么你就能够与圣人同名。

7. It is very easy to forgive others their mistakes; it takes more grit and gumption to forgive them for having witnessed your own.
要原谅犯错的人很简单，反而是对那些见证了你的错误的人，就需要些智慧与勇气了。

8. About morals, I know only that what is moral is what you feel

good after and what is immoral is what you feel bad after.
关于道德，我只知道美德能让你事后感觉身心愉快，而罪恶则总会让你自责不已。

9. Every man's life ends the same way. It is only the details of how he lived and how he died that distinguish one man from another.
每个人的人生都以同样的方式结束。人与人的区别在于他是如何生活与死去的。

读书笔记

32 Nights
夜晚

Night has fallen over the country. Through the trees rises the red moon and the stars are **scarcely** seen. In the vast shadow of night the coolness and the **dews** descend. I sit at the open window to enjoy them; and hear only the voice of the summer wind. Like black **hulks,** the shadows of the great trees ride at **anchor** on the **billowy** sea of grass. I cannot see the red and blue flowers, but I know that they are there. Far away in the **meadow** gleams the silver Charles. The **tramp** of horses' **hoofs** sounds from the wooden bridge. Then all is still save the continuous wind or the sound of the neighboring sea. The village clock strikes; and I feel that I am not alone.

How different it is in the city! It is late, and the crowd is gone. You step out upon the **balcony**, and lie in the very bosom of the cool, dewy night as if you folded her garments about you. Beneath lies the public walk with trees, like a **fathomless,** black gulf. The lamps are still burning up and down the long street. People go by with **grotesque** shadows, now foreshortened, and now

夜幕已经笼罩乡间。一轮红月正从树林后面徐徐升起，天上几乎见不到星星。在这苍茫的夜色中，寒气与露水降下来了。我坐在敞开的窗前欣赏着这夜色，耳边只听见那夏天的风声。大树的阴影像黑色的大船停泊在波浪起伏的茫茫草海上。我看不到红色和蓝色的花，但我知道它们在那里。远处的草地上，银色的查尔斯河闪闪发光。木桥那边传来了踢踏踢踏的马蹄声。然后仍然是接连不断的风声和附近大海的声音。村子里的时钟敲起来了，我觉得并不孤单。

在城市里是多么不同啊！很晚了，人群已经散去。你走到阳台上，躺在凉爽和露水弥漫的夜幕中，仿佛你用它作为外衣裹住了你的身子。阳台下面是栽着树木的人行道，像一条深不可测的黑色的海湾。长长的街道上，街灯依然到处亮着。人们从灯下走过，拖着各种各样奇形怪状的影子，时而缩短，时而延长，走进黑暗中然后消失，同时，一个新的影

lengthening away into the darkness and vanishing, while a new one springs up behind the walker, and seems to pass him revolving like the sail of a windmill. The iron gates of the park shut with a jangling clang. There are footsteps and loud voices: a **tumult**, a drunken **brawl**, an alarm of fire, then silence again. And now at length the city is asleep, and we can see the night. The belated moon looks over the roofs, and finds no one to welcome her. The moonlight is broken. It lies here and there in the squares, and the opening of the streets.

子又突然出现在那个行路人的身后，这影子似像风车上的翼板一样，转到他身体的前方去了。公园的铁门当啷一声关上。耳边可以听到脚步声和响亮的说话声：一阵喧闹，一阵酒醉后的吵嚷声，一阵火灾的报警声。接着，寂静如初。于是，城市终于沉睡，我们终于能够看到夜的景色。姗姗来迟的月亮从屋顶后面探出脸来，发觉没有人在欢迎她。月光破碎，洒在各处，洒在广场，洒在街道上。

单词解析 Word Analysis

scarcely ['skersli] *adv.* 几乎不；简直不；刚刚；决不

例 He spoke scarcely a word of English.
他几乎连一个英文单词都不会说。

dew [duː] *n.* 露水

例 The dew on the grass drizzled my shoes.
草上的露水打湿了我的鞋。

hulk [hʌlk] *n.* 废船；笨重的人或物

例 I saw a rotting hulk on the beach.
我在海滩上看见了一艘腐烂的废船。

anchor ['æŋkər] *n.* 锚；锚状物；依靠；新闻节目主播；压阵队员

例 The ship dragged its anchor during the night.
夜里，船把锚拖动了。

Nights 夜晚

billowy [ˈbɪloʊɪ] *adj* 波涛汹涌的；巨浪般的；巨浪的
例 One billowy river appeared in front of the Cowhand.
牛郎面前出现一条波涛汹涌的天河。

meadow [ˈmedoʊ] *n.* 草地；牧场
例 Cattle were grazing on the meadow.
牛在牧场上吃草。

tramp [træmp] *v.* 徒步；践踏 *n.* 徒步；流浪汉；沉重的脚步声
例 She wants to go for a tramp in the country.
她想去乡间远足。

hoof [huːf] *n.* 蹄；<俚>人的脚
例 She tried very hard and finally she was able to write her name with her hoof.
她很努力地设法写，终能用她的脚写出她的名字。

balcony [ˈbælkəni] *n.* 阳台；楼座；包厢
例 The prospect from the balcony was breathtaking.
从阳台上看去景色美极了。

fathomless [ˈfæðəmlɪs] *adj* 深不可测的；不能理解的
例 Days are colored bubbles that float upon the surface of fathomless night.
白天是彩色的泡沫浮动在深不可测的夜的表面上。

grotesque [groʊˈtesk] *adj* 奇形怪状的；奇怪的；怪诞的；可笑的
例 The most grotesque and fantastic conceits haunted him in his bed at night.
夜晚躺在床上的时候，各种离奇怪诞的幻想纷至沓来。

tumult [ˈtuːmʌlt] *v.* 骚乱；嘈杂声；烦乱
例 Presently the tumult died down.
一会儿工夫骚动平息了下来。

brawl [brɔːl] *v.* 争吵；大声地吵闹
例 He shall not get so angry. What we have gotten here is more like

a brawl than a debate.
他不应该那么生气的。这里的样子不像在讨论而像是在吵架。

语法知识点 *Grammar points*

① You step out upon the balcony, and lie in the very bosom of the cool, dewy night as if you folded her garments about you.

step out 走出去；暂时离开，跳出

例 They stepped out of the sun into the coolness.
他们到阴凉处躲避烈日。

lie in 在于；睡懒觉

例 It's a holiday tomorrow, so you can lie in.
明天是假日，你可以睡懒觉了。

as if 犹如，好像，好似，仿佛

例 After the rain the corn shot up as if by magic.
雨后，玉米苗像变魔术一般的长起来了。

② The lamps are still burning up and down the long street. People go by with grotesque shadows, now foreshortened, and now lengthening away into the darkness and vanishing, while a new one springs up behind the walker, and seems to pass him revolving like the sail of a windmill.

burn up 烧起来；烧尽；（使）发怒

例 All the wood has been burnt up.
木柴全部烧光了。

go by （时间）过去，逝去，消逝；经过；走过；依照；错过

例 He can drive his car to work or go by bus.
他可以自己驾车上班或乘公车。

It's not always wise to go by appearances.
根据表面现象看问题有时是不可取的。

spring up 跳起；发生；萌芽；出现

例 Doubts have begun to spring up in my mind.
我心里充满了怀疑。

New houses are springing up all over the city.
新建筑物犹如雨后春笋般地出现在这座城市里。

③ **And now at length the city is asleep, and we can see the night. The belated moon looks over the roofs, and finds no one to welcome her.**

at length 终于；最后；详细地；详尽地

例 We will debate the subject at length later when we are at leisure.
我们等有空再对这题目展开辩论。

The sea was gradually gaining on the buildings, which at length almost entirely disappeared.
大海不断地侵蚀着这些建筑物，最后它们几乎不见了。

look over 检查；查看；调查

例 If you do harm to me, I shall not look over you.
如你对我使坏，我可不饶恕你。

例 We must look over all the accounts today.
我们今天必须审查一下所有的账目。

经典名句 *Famous Classics*

1. Most people die at the last minute; others twenty years beforehand, some even earlier. They are the wretched of the earth.
大多数人在最后一刻才死去；其他人在那之前的二十年就死去了；有些人甚至还要提前，他们是这个世界上非常不幸的人。

2. The only basis for living is believing in life, loving it, and applying the whole force of one's intellect to know it better.
生活只能建立在对生命的信仰之上，要热爱生命并且竭尽自己的智慧去更加懂得生命。

3. Happiness is beneficial for the body, but it is grief that develops the powers of the mind.
快乐有利于身体健康，但是悲痛才给了我们精神上的力量。

4. It is often said that there is no such thing as a free lunch, the universe, however, is a "free lunch".

人们总说没有免费的午餐，但是整个宇宙对我们都是"免费的午餐"。

5. Half our life is spent trying to find something to do with the time we have rushed through life trying to save.
终其一生我们都在匆匆忙忙地试图留住时间，而我们也往往花费半生来思考该用这些时间干些什么。

6. Men talk of killing time, while time quietly kills them.
人们常说要消磨时间，而时间也慢慢地消磨了人们。

7. Our life is frittered away by detail…Simplify, simplify.
我们的人生被琐碎之事消耗至尽……简化一些吧！

8. Expect nothing. Live frugally on surprise.
不要去期待任何事情，靠惊喜为生吧。

9. Life is a gamble at terrible odds—if it was a bet, you wouldn't take it.
生命是一场没什么胜算的赌注，如果可以的话，不要下赌。

10. Believe me! The secret of reaping the greatest fruitfulness and the greatest enjoyment from life is to live dangerously!
相信我吧！从生命中获得最多成果与快乐的方法，就是危险地活着。

11. Science offers the best answers to the meaning of life. Science offers the privilege of understanding before you die why you were ever born in the first place.
科学可以为生命的意义提供最好的解释。科学让我们在离开这个世界前，得以明白自己是怎样地来到世界上。

12. The spirit of self-help is the root of all genuine growth in the individual.
自助的精神能够帮助一个人真正的成长。

13. We're all of us sentenced to solitary confinement inside our own skins, for life!
我们都被判决要孤独地居住在自己的身体里，这种判决是终身的！

33 The Hard Work Paid Off
天道酬勤

Louis Caldera, recalling his first job experience: the parking-lot sweeper, was the 17th Secretary of the Army of the U. S. A.

His parents **imbued** in him the **concepts** of family, faith and **patriotism** when Louis Caldera was young. Even though they **struggled** to make ends meet, they stressed to him and his four brothers and sisters how **fortunate** they were to live in a great country with **limitless** opportunities.

He got his first real job when he was ten. His dad, Benjamin, injured his back working in a **cardboard-box** factory and was retrained as a **hairstylist**. He rented space in a little strip mall and gave his shop the fancy name of Mr. Ben's Coiffure.

The owner of the shopping center gave his Dad a **discount** on his rent for cleaning the parking lot three nights a week, which meant getting up at 3 A. M. to pick up **trash**, Dad used a little machine that looked like a lawn **mower**. His Mom and he **emptied** garbage cans and picked up litter by hand. It took two to three hours to clean the lot. He'd sleep in the car on the way home.

路易斯·卡尔德是美国军队第17届秘书长，他回忆起了自己的第一份工作——停车场的清洁员。

尽管他们挣扎度日，勉强维持收支平衡，但他的父母仍然对他和他的4个兄弟姐妹强调他们多么幸运，能够生活在一个充满无限机遇的伟大国家里。向他们灌输家庭、信念和爱国精神的观念。

10岁的时候，他得到了第一份真正的工作。他的父亲本杰明在一家纸箱厂工作的时候，后背受伤了，他学习成为一名美发师。他在一条商业小街上租了一个地方，给自己的店铺起了一个奇特的名字——本先生发型店。

商业街的业主在租金上给他爸爸打了折，条件是每周3个晚上清理停车场，那就意味着要在凌晨3点起床。他爸爸用一部看上去像割草机一样的机器来收垃圾；他和妈妈倾倒垃圾桶，用手来捡垃圾。清理这个停车场需要用2至3小时。在回家的路上，他睡在车上。

He did this for two years, but the lessons he learned have lasted a lifetime. He acquired **discipline** and a strong work **ethic**, and learned at an early age the importance of balancing life's competing interests, in my case, school, homework and a job. This really helped during his senior year of high school, when he worked 40 hours a week flipping burgers at a fast-food joint while taking a full load of college-prep courses.

The hard work paid off. He attended the U. S. Military Academy and went on to receive graduate degrees in law and business from Harvard. Later, he joined a big Los Angeles law firm and was elected to the California state assembly. In these jobs and in everything else he has done, he has never forgotten those nights in the parking lot. The experience taught him that there is **dignity** in all work and that if people are working to provide for themselves and their families, that is something we should **honor**.

这个工作他做了两年，但学到的东西却使他受益一生。他养成了自律性和坚定的工作道德，并小小年纪就懂得了在有冲突的生活利益——他自己的事情、学校、家务和工作之间掌握平衡的重要性。在他中学的最后一年期间，这真的对他有很大帮助，当时他正在学习全部大学预科课程，准备考大学，与此同时，他每周还要工作40小时，在一家快餐连锁店做汉堡。

艰苦的努力获得了丰厚的回报。他考上了美国陆军军官学校，继而取得了哈佛大学的法律和商业硕士学位。后来，他进入了洛杉矶一家很大的法律公司，并当选为加州议员。在做这些工作以及其他任何事情的时候，他从未忘记过清理停车场的那些夜晚。那些经历使他懂得，所有的工作都有尊严，只要是自食其力、能够养家糊口的人，都应该受到尊敬。

单词解析 *Word Analysis*

imbue [ɪmˈbjuː] 灌输

例 As you listen, you notice how every single word is imbued with a breathless sense of wonder.
你仔细听，就会注意到每一个词都是那么的神奇，令人惊叹。

concept ['kɒnsept] *n.* 概念；观念
- She added that the concept of arranged marriages is misunderstood in the west.
  她补充说，西方人对包办婚姻的概念有些误解。

struggle ['strʌgl] *v.* 奋力，努力，尽力；挣扎，努力挣脱
- They had to struggle against all kinds of adversity.
  他们不得不同一切困境做斗争。
- I struggled, but he was a tall man, well-built.
  我使劲挣扎，但他又高又壮。

fortunate ['fɔːtʃənət] *adj.* 幸运的；有幸的
- He was extremely fortunate to survive.
  他能活下来真是万幸。
- Central London is fortunate in having so many large parks and open spaces.
  伦敦市中心有幸拥有许多大型公园和大片空地。

limitless ['lɪmɪtləs] *adj.* 无限的；无穷无尽的
- The opportunities are limitless.
  机会无限。

cardboard-box 硬纸板盒
- She brought the shopping home in a cardboard box.
  她将买的东西放在纸箱里带回家。

hairstylist ['heəstaɪlɪst] *n.* 发型设计师
- She put complete faith in her hairstylist.
  她完全信任自己的发型师。

discount ['dɪskaʊnt] *n.* 减价，打折
- They are often available at a discount.
  它们经常进行打折销售。

trash [træʃ] *n.* 垃圾，废物；断枝，碎块；废话；社会渣滓
- The yards are overgrown and cluttered with trash.
  院子里杂草丛生，垃圾成堆。

mower ['məʊə(r)] *n.* 割草机；割草的人
- Your big lawn mower is just the job for the high grass.
  割高草时正需要你的大割草机。

empty ['empti] *v.* （使）成为空的，把……弄空；把……腾出来
- Empty the noodles and liquid into a serving bowl.
  把汤面倒进上菜用的碗中。

discipline ['dɪsəplɪn] *n.* 训练；纪律；学科
- Order and discipline have been placed in the hands of headmasters and governing bodies.
  维持秩序和纪律的工作已交接给了校长和管理机构了。

ethic ['eθɪk] *n.* 道德规范；伦理
- Its members are bound by a rigid code of ethics which includes confidentiality.
  它的成员受到包括保密在内的一套严格的伦理规范的约束。

dignity ['dɪgnəti] *n.* 尊严；高尚；自豪；自尊
- If you were wrong, admit it. You won't lose dignity, but will gain respect.
  如果你错了，那就承认。你不会因此而失去尊严，反而会赢得尊重。

honor *n.* 尊敬；光荣；节操；荣誉
- It's quite an honor to have two men fighting over me.
  有两个人争着要我，我感到很荣幸。

语法知识点 *Grammar points*

① Even though they struggled to make ends meet, they stressed to him and his four brothers and sisters how fortunate they were to live in a great country with limitless opportunities.

make ends meet 使收支相抵

例 But municipal Wi-Fi schemes have been struggling to make ends meet.
但是，城市 Wi-Fi计划为了维持收支平衡，正在艰难挣扎。
It may be difficult at times to make ends meet on your small income.
靠你微薄的收入做到收支相抵，有时可能是困难的。

② **It took two to three hours to clean the lot. He'd sleep in the car on the way home.**

It takes some time to do sth. 花费时间做某事

例 It took Susan two hours to finish her homework last night.
昨晚苏珊花了两个小时做完了她的家庭作业。

③ **The experience taught him that there is dignity in all work and that if people are working to provide for themselves and their families, that is something we should honor.**

此句子结构是：The experience taught sb. that... and that if... that（代词）...动词taught后接了由that引导的两个宾语从句，第二个that引导的宾语从句中是一个含有if条件状语从句的复合句。

经典名句 Famous Classics

1. Life is like playing a violin solo in public and learning the instrument as one goes on.
生活就像是一边学习演奏，一边当众演奏小提琴。

2. What is called the serenity of age is only perhaps a euphemism for the fading power to feel the sudden shock of joy or sorrow.
上了年纪的人所谓的冷静沉着，也许只是一种委婉说法。实际上是因为他们对欢乐与悲伤的感知能力衰退了。

3. As you pass from the tender years of youth into harsh and embittered manhood, make sure you take with you on your

journey all the human emotions! Don't leave them on the road, for you will not pick them up afterwards!
在你从敏感的青春走向残酷现实的成年时，记得在这途中带好你全部的情感！不要把他们丢在路上，因为以后你就无法将他们捡回来了！

4. An adventure is only an inconvenience rightly considered. An inconvenience is only an adventure wrongly considered.
   正确地认识你的麻烦，它就成了一场冒险。如果你不能正视一场冒险，它就变成了一堆麻烦。

5. I postpone death by living, by suffering, by error, by risking, by giving.
   我用生活、痛苦、错误、冒险与奉献——来拖延死亡。

6. The humorous man recognizes that absolute purity, absolute justice, absolute logic and perfection are beyond human achievement and that men have been able to live happily for thousands of years in a state of genial frailty.
   有幽默感的人明白，绝对的纯净、绝对的公平、绝对的逻辑以及完美是人类无法企及的，人类在平凡与脆弱中，已经欣然存活了上万年。

7. Life is the greatest bargain; we get it for nothing.
   生命是一笔再划算不过的交易，我们免费得到了它。

读书笔记